T0279074

PROM BABIES

PROM BABIES

Kekla
Magoon

HENRY HOLT AND COMPANY
NEW YORK

Henry Holt and Company, *Publishers since 1866*

Henry Holt® is a registered trademark of Macmillan Publishing Group, LLC

120 Broadway, New York, NY 10271 • fiercereads.com

Our books may be purchased in bulk for promotional, educational, or
business use. Please contact your local bookseller or the Macmillan
Corporate and Premium Sales Department at (800) 221-7945 ext. 5442 or
by email at MacmillanSpecialMarkets@macmillan.com.

Library of Congress Cataloging-in-Publication Data

Names: Magoon, Kekla, author.
Title: Prom babies / Kekla Magoon.
Description: First. | New York : Henry Holt Books and Company,
2024. | Audience: Ages 14–18. | Audience: Grades 10–12. |
Summary: "A multi-generational novel beginning with three teen
girls who become pregnant on prom night, and picking up as their
three teens head to prom eighteen years later"—Provided
by publisher.
Identifiers: LCCN 2023030408 | ISBN 9781250806253 (hardcover)
Subjects: CYAC: Proms—Fiction. | Pregnancy—Fiction. | High
schools—Fiction. | Schools—Fiction. | African Americans—Fiction.
Classification: LCC PZ7.M2739 Pr 2024 | DDC [Fic]—dc23
LC record available at https://lccn.loc.gov/2023030408

First edition, 2024

Book design by Julia Bianchi

Printed in the United States of America by Lakeside Book Company,
Harrisonburg, Virginia

ISBN 978-1-250-80625-3 (hardcover)

1   3   5   7   9   10   8   6   4   2

ALSO BY KEKLA MAGOON

The Rock and the River

37 Things I Love (in No Particular Order)

Fire in the Streets

How It Went Down

X: A Novel

Light It Up

*Revolution in Our Time: The Black Panther Party's
Promise to the People*

The Minus-One Club

PRAISE FOR KEKLA MAGOON

★ "This timely and thoughtful novel makes room for the increasing depth and complexity of navigating adolescence alongside grief, religious dissent, and healing."

—BOOKLIST, starred review for *The Minus-One Club*

"Brilliantly crafted, heart-wrenching, and unforgettable."

—LAURIE HALSE ANDERSON, *New York Times*–bestselling author of *Speak* on *How It Went Down*

★ "This gritty, emotional tale will leave readers gutted and compelled to stand against flawed systems."

—PUBLISHERS WEEKLY, starred review for *Light It Up*

For Cyn, in gratitude for her
support and inspiration

THEN
April 2005

*"My mom once told me,
'Just watch, you'll end up pregnant at
eighteen like I did, and then your life will be over.'
I swore it would never happen. Not like that. Not like
Mom. And I was right. I was seventeen."*

— Penney Rutledge

*"He was so cute. Star of the football team. I know.
It's totally cliché, right? But what are you supposed to
do in the face of those biceps? Those glutes. He knew how to
dress, too, so he always looked amazing. It wasn't even our
first time. And we were really careful. I mean, come on.
It wasn't even our first time."*

— Mina Morgan

"Some moments change everything."

— Sheryl Brewster

Penney

Prom night was supposed to be special. Everyone said so. Penney was hoping for special in a lights-and-fireworks kind of way, but it showed up different than that.

The evening started out great. It seemed like all the stars were aligning to give her the perfect night. At 4:15 p.m. precisely, she knocked on the alley door at the back of the mall's Sephora.

The door creaked open. "Hey, babe," said Janice, Penney's mom's best friend. "Come on in."

Penney followed her into the storage room, which was filled with stacks of shipping boxes from all kinds of fancy makeup and skin care brands.

"We lucked out," Janice said. "The manager had to go upstairs to meet with corporate. That always takes forever, which means we can go out front and do this proper."

"Cool," Penney said. She would have been happy to have a professional makeup job any way she could get it, but she got an extra little thrill at the idea of posing in front of mirrors and lights instead of crouching in the storeroom.

They came out behind the counter and nodded at the sales-clerks they passed. Sephora was always busy and they had a million staffers roaming around making product recommendations and handing out adorable little baskets to the shoppers so that they could buy even more stuff. Penney could not shop here herself because everything was so expensive. She was more of a corner drugstore kind of girl when it came to everyday makeup, and she didn't even wear all that much unless she was working. It was true that pretty waitresses got better tips, so all of Penney's work clothes were carefully chosen for fit as well.

"Hop up here." Janice patted a tall stool at the makeup demo counter. The mirrors were huge and lit by a frame of small bulbs. The surface of the table contained samples in every color of eye shadow and lip stain you could imagine.

Penney settled onto the padded stool, which looked awfully similar to the counter stools at the diner, yet somehow cushioned her butt in a fancier way. "This is amazing. Thanks."

Janice's hands worked swiftly, color-matching Penney's foundation and accent color scheme. The dress she was going to wear was so fancy that it had come with a small swatch of fabric attached to the tag that you could carry around when you went shoe or accessory shopping. Penney pulled it out now. Janice nodded, using it to select a complementary gold sparkly eye shadow.

"Now, this foundation is going to do wonders for your complexion in the long run," Janice said. "Coupled with that luscious primer, oh my god, I swear, you'll never go back . . ." She chatted enthusiastically at Penney the whole time she worked, describing the products and their various benefits, like she was genuinely trying to make a sale. Penney played her part, oohing and aahing over the colors and marveling at the transformation. She didn't have to work hard to marvel, honestly. Sitting here under the lights, she felt like a goddamn princess.

When Penney got home, her mom was waiting. Rhonda stood at the kitchen door, blowing smoke from her cigarette out the screen. She nodded as Penney approached. "Glad to see Janice did you right."

Penney smiled at the rare compliment from her mom. Rhonda was a matter-of-fact person who never went out of her way to be flowery. Even this kind statement was delivered in an "it is what it is" tone of voice.

"Sit at the table," Rhonda said. Penney did. The table was laid out with products and supplies borrowed from their hairstylist neighbor.

Rhonda stubbed out her cigarette in the ashtray on the counter and got to work. She stuck a foam cylinder to the back of Penney's head and swept her long dark-blond hair up around it in a swirl. She fluffed and arched Penney's bangs to give them volume and shape.

Rhonda shook the aerosol hair spray can. "Close your eyes." Penney did.

The spraying sound seemed to go on forever. A cloud of mist settled on her neck and shoulders, causing a tiny shiver. When it was quiet again, Penney opened her eyes.

Rhonda surveyed her handiwork. "That'll do." She patted Penney's back and stalked out of the room.

Penney had saved up several weeks of tips to buy a dress she loved. She'd cut the tag off and everything. This was a keeper. If she stayed on track and went to college like Colby was always encouraging her to, maybe she could wear it again to another formal. At the very least, she'd be the splashiest chick in the room at the next handful of weddings she went to.

The fabric was a sparkly gold. The saleswoman at the department store had called the style a "mermaid cut." The dress was one-shoulder, fitted through the bodice and hips. The shape narrowed dramatically below the hips, clinging to her legs, but then the bottom few inches near the hem were made of gauzy gold tulle that flared out again. It flattered Penney's tall and shapely but not-too-thin frame. Her strappy heeled sandals were a thrift store find. A little glitter and glue had perked them right up.

Colby would be here in less than twenty minutes. He was always on time, sometimes early. Penney went to the bathroom for a final time before donning the dress. She slipped into the lacy matching bra and panties she'd chosen for the occasion. They had cost almost as much as the dress, for crying out loud, but she and Colby had a private after-prom party planned and she wanted it to be special.

When Penney returned to the kitchen, she found her mother had dug out their camera and brushed the dust off.

"Can't let you leave looking so nice without a picture, now can I?"

Wow, she was two for two on compliments today.

"Thanks, Mom."

Rhonda brushed it off. "It's prom. If we're doing it, we're doing it, right?"

Penney grinned. "Right."

Rhonda raised the camera and clicked.

Colby arrived a few minutes later. Rhonda opened the door for him, and he made it about three steps inside before his jaw dropped and his eyes nearly bugged out of his head.

"Wow," he managed finally. "I mean, you . . . wow . . . wow."

Penney burst forward and kissed him. "Thanks," she said. His reaction was above and beyond what she'd been hoping for. The glow that had come over her under the makeup lights intensified.

Rhonda snapped a few pictures of the couple. "The light is better out front," she said. So they went onto the porch and took a few pictures next to the bush beside the driveway. It had pretty purple flowers that were just budding this time of year.

In the driveway, Colby surprised her with a corsage of flowers. He'd asked her dress color, and so the flowers were delicate white and pale yellow with one red blossom in the center. It didn't quite match her dress, honestly, but the thought was what mattered. It was going to look just fine.

"Thanks," Penney said. "I wasn't expecting flowers, you know. They're so expensive."

"They're from my neighbor's yard." Colby laughed self-deprecatingly. "She has a lot of flowers and she said it was all right."

"You made this yourself?" Penney was genuinely surprised. When she looked closely, she could see the stems were wrapped with what appeared to be a shoelace. "In that case, it's super impressive."

He'd made a boutonniere for himself to match, and so they pinned them on each other ceremoniously.

Like Penney, Colby didn't have a lot of cash to spare. He worked part-time at a farm outside of town, and his Ghanaian parents wished he wouldn't even do that so he could focus on his studies. But he was at the top of his class and had already been admitted to Purdue's school of engineering with a full academic merit scholarship. He was going to build something that would change the world, Penney was sure of it.

"No one's going to recognize us," Colby commented as he helped her into the cab of his Chevy Silverado.

Penney laughed. "You're a regular Superman."

Colby grinned and mock-loosened his bow tie, as though to transform.

"Does that make me Lois Lane?"

"You write well enough." Colby leaned in and kissed her. "Your op-ed on the economic inequities of prom culture was really great."

"Stop." Penney blushed. "It was a spur-of-the-moment thing. I was just mad that they made the tickets so expensive. You're the only one who liked the article even a little bit."

"I bet that's not true," Colby said, climbing into the cab. "The people who liked it can't tell you they liked it for exactly the reason you talk about in the article. It's embarrassing to admit what you can't afford."

"Yeah, I guess. But all I've been hearing all week is a lot of 'why can't you shut up and enjoy the dance?' from the pretty people." She sighed.

"Anyway, we got it done, didn't we? Come hell or high water."

"Damn straight." They high-fived across the Silverado cab, and Colby pulled out of the driveway.

Fuck all the haters. It was their prom too.

Mina

"Close your eyes," the makeup artist said.

Mina did. A light spritz of mist settled over her face.

"Can you believe prom is finally here?" Taylor asked, from alongside her. "It feels like we've been preparing for a hundred years."

"Totally," Mina said. Taylor had a tendency to exaggerate, but in this case, she definitely agreed. They'd been pointed toward prom like the North Star for over a month now.

"Okay, open," the makeup artist said. "All done."

"Thanks." Mina studied her appearance in the mirror. She didn't look like herself. The makeup was nice, if a little more dramatic than she usually went for. It was the straightened hair swept into its updo that felt awkward. The hairstylist had been surprised to encounter Black hair among the group of four friends who'd booked her for prom prep.

Mina touched the twin tendrils that framed her face. They'd been straightened, re-curled, and sprayed to within an inch of their life. They hung there like icicles.

Thirty minutes ago, the hairstylist had frowned and fretted as she lifted Mina's shoulder-length curls. "It could be so pretty," she'd cooed, "but I really don't have time to straighten it all out."

No one asked you to, Mina thought. She was biracial. Curly hair was kind of a given, and she wore her hair natural despite its challenges because her mother had always insisted. She had come pre-washed and moisturized. Even on their own, her curls were popping. She'd figured the stylist would pin them up in some cool way to show off their texture.

Instead, the stylist had gathered the center mass of Mina's curls into a bun-like coil at the back of her head, then straightened the outer layers of hair and swept them in and up to cover the rest. She felt like a bride out of a 1990s magazine. It was pretty, it just wasn't *her*. Maybe she should have stopped it at the start, but she'd been too awkward or embarrassed to ask for something different. Going with the flow was just easier.

"Squee!" Taylor clapped her hands as the stylist held the hand mirror up so she could see the finished hairdo, which was nearly identical. It was definitely a style made for hair like Taylor's, not hair like Mina's.

Avery hopped up off the bed and nudged Mina out of the chair. "My turn," she said. Joan switched places with Taylor, and the second half of the styling session began.

Between the four of them, it had been affordable to hire a stylist and makeup artist to come to the house instead of going to the salon. They were at Taylor's, because she had the biggest bedroom. Their tailored dresses hung neatly in the closet, ready and waiting. They'd spent the morning getting mani-pedis in the perfect colors and the early afternoon finalizing their jewelry choices.

"This is the best day ever," Joan gushed as the hairstylist brandished the curling iron over her like a magic wand. "I still can't believe that I'm going with Troy." She practically squealed his name, in a mix of panic and excitement.

"Please." Avery rolled her eyes. "Who else was he going to ask?"

Ouch. Mina's eyes widened. Joan was the perpetually single one in their friend group, and Troy was her single parallel from the guys' side, because he grew up besties with Avery's boyfriend. But Joan had had a crush on him forever.

"Avery," Taylor scolded. "Oh, my god."

Avery laughed. "I meant it as, you know, who else would he realistically like? It's logical for him to be into you," she said reassuringly.

Joan blinked toward the mirror. "I know he might have just asked me as a friend, okay?" she said softly. "But it's still technically a date, and I'm still going to enjoy it."

Mina admired her for saying that out loud. "He's always been shy," she added, hoping to help. "Maybe he needed the pressure of prom to find the courage to ask you out. Stay positive."

"I will." Joan smiled at her in the mirror. "I only wish I was less shy myself, and I could just walk up to him and declare how I feel, like you did with Chip. Boom! Instant boyfriend."

Mina stopped herself from blurting *Chip isn't my boyfriend.* Because of course, he technically was. They spent weekends together. They had sex. She went to his football games and let him drape his sweaty arm around her when she congratulated him afterward. But it was mostly those things, between them. Low-key hangouts, someone to do stuff with who you can also kiss. It had been a year and it was still somehow nothing serious. They had fun together, no question, but she also didn't have any of the gut-churning eagerness she read on Joan's face right now. It wasn't the deep, vulnerable love connection that Joan was suggesting it to be.

Mina shifted uncomfortably as these thoughts flashed through her. "Well, remember, all I really did was ask if he wanted to go to a movie," she reminded Joan now. "You could do that too. End of the night, when he drops you off, just toss it out there."

"Hey, would you want to go to a movie sometime?" Joan

practiced. She did a little wave of her hand that was both sexy and casual.

"Exactly." Mina smiled. "See? You're a natural."

"And do the hand thing, exactly like that," Avery suggested. "That was hot."

Joan blushed. They all laughed.

Their dates would arrive in an hour. They'd stand on Taylor's deck, overlooking the perfectly manicured lawn and garden, and take group and couple pictures. They had dinner reservations for a party of eight at the steak house. Everything was shaping up to be as perfect as they'd planned.

Sheryl

The dress fit perfectly, which still surprised her since it was borrowed.

She'd agreed to go to prom on a whim, basically. She hadn't been expecting an invitation or even hoping for one. The foster kids in school, they sorta tried to stick together, you know? And few of them could afford a prom ticket, let alone all the extras like tuxedo rentals, boutonnieres, and restaurant dinners. So they'd planned a kind of anti-prom, dressing up as far as they could for free, snacking on chips and beer in someone's borrowed basement. It would be a dance party, of sorts, if not too dissimilar from a normal Saturday night. Maybe someone would bring some streamers to decorate, or they could light sparklers or something.

But when the cool and popular Rob Clayton asked if she wanted to go to the real prom, and he did that awkward foot shuffling thing guys do when they really hope you'll say yes . . . she caved. It's not like she had to buy a dress or anything. The bedroom closet in the house where she was staying now had a lot of size-ten dresses, several of which were a decent-enough fit for Sheryl to get away with wearing. She'd simply chosen one for the night, certain it wouldn't be missed.

She'd gotten her hair trimmed earlier in the week. Today, she washed and blow dried it as well as she could. She didn't have any fancy cosmetology skills to speak of, though as someone who enjoyed painting, she had a better understanding of makeup than hair. She had decently pretty brown waves, if she did say so herself, so hopefully wearing her hair down would be all right.

She'd done her best on the makeup. It looked okay, she figured. She'd also torn a perfume sample out of a magazine in the dentist's office waiting area last week. Now she pulled it open and rubbed it against her wrists and throat. It smelled nice. Classy.

Rob climbed onto the porch at five past six. Sheryl opened the door for him, already breathless.

"You look great," he said, flashing his thousand-watt smile. "Lucky me."

"So do you." Rob could wear a tux, that was for sure.

He leaned forward and kissed her cheek. He smelled like expensive aftershave. The skin of his chiseled jaw was surprisingly soft. "That dress is dreamy," he whispered in her ear.

Sheryl flushed with pleasure. Going to prom with Rob Clayton was a dream to begin with. They were science lab partners, but they didn't exactly run in the same circles socially. He was one of the most handsome guys in school. He should have had his pick of dates, but he had chosen her. She'd pinched herself under the desk when he asked.

"I thought you had a girlfriend," she'd said, like a doofus.

"Not at the moment." He'd shrugged, then spider-walked his fingers across the tabletop until they drummed gently against her wrist. "So, what do you say?"

Looking into his warm blue eyes, Sheryl knew there was only one right answer.

Now, as Rob helped her into his Acura, it occurred to her that she'd never been on a proper date. There had been a boy or two of interest over the years, but just barely. In eighth grade, she'd held hands with Paulo in the beanbag chairs corner of the library during quiet reading time. That had lasted about a week. In tenth, she'd gone mini golfing with this guy Steve from the group home. She'd grown up mini golfing because her mom had worked at the place for a while, but she still let him put his arms around her and "show" her how to swing. But they'd met there and she'd walked home alone after he bumped into some school friends and ditched her. Last year, she'd made out with Chad behind the Baptist church on a few Sundays, until she moved foster homes and didn't have to go to church every week anymore.

She'd never been picked up and driven out to a nice restaurant, the way people did in the movies. But here they were, driving toward the Olive Garden and chatting about their shared love of the new hospital series *Grey's Anatomy*.

Rob had the windows cracked, which stirred her hair, but the breeze felt nice so she didn't really mind. Windblown was supposed to be sexy, right?

When they got there, he hopped out and held the car door for her. He put his hand on her waist as they crossed the parking lot. No one had ever done that before. The surety of it surprised her. It was like leaning on a wall, if a wall could also propel you forward with ease and confidence.

She turned her head and smiled up at him. Her foster mom had offered her twenty-five dollars for the night—just enough to cover an Olive Garden entrée, tax, and tip. "If he's a gentleman, he should pay for you," Mrs. Jones had said. "This is just in case."

She wasn't worried. Rob was a gentleman. He had paid for their tickets and he'd even paid for the expected corsage and boutonniere. She could have chipped in a little, but she might have chosen not to go instead. Rob knew she had been saving up her allowance and odd-job money all year so she'd have some cash in the fall when she got to college.

But she had to admit, there was something about having a few spendable bucks in her pocket that made it all feel so much better. She could at least offer to pay for her own meal, which meant she could relax. She wasn't beholden to him.

Rob squeezed her hip. "I don't know," he said, shaking his head. "When you smile at me like that, it makes me want to skip the dance entirely."

Sheryl laughed. Obviously, he was joking. He'd spent so much money on the tickets. They couldn't go to waste.

His hand tightened around her hip again. "This is gonna be an amazing night."

Sheryl smiled again. "It's already amazing."

Penney

The dance itself was all they'd hoped it would be, and more. For hours, in the throng, Penney pressed her hands against the sky and danced with abandon, Colby's hands never far from her hips, reminding her of what was to come. Teasing it. Promising.

The dance ended at ten, which gave them plenty of time for a private excursion.

Now they were on the bed in some cheap hotel and Colby had bought this cheap bottle of hooch. It burned going down, but it had a sweet aftertaste. They had a couple of sips. Nothing major. They weren't even drunk, really, just glowing with the sense of freedom and adulthood that came with having a bottle on the nightstand. It was still mostly full. Penney and Colby weren't into escapism—at least not like that—but they were over the moon into each other.

She pressed her hands against the headboard, making way for Colby to do his work on her half-naked body. He kissed her, caressed her. She closed her eyes and arched her back into it.

He was squeezing her boobs a little too much, though. "Gentler," Penney breathed, grasping his wrist to help soften his touch. After some awkwardness in their first few times together, she had learned that it was okay to say what she wanted, not simply put up with whatever he tried. Colby made her feel safe to speak her mind, and that was important.

"Like this?" he panted, adjusting.

"Yeah," she said. "Better." And it was. It was great.

God, he was hot. Penney's whole body thrummed with excitement. Prom had thrilled her to no end, but this took the cake. A dance all their own. No one watching, or judging.

They'd done it once already, and it was perfect. But with another whole hour stretching before them, not to mention the heat of it all, why the hell not batter up for round two?

"Shit," Colby said a few minutes later.

"What?" Penney opened her eyes.

"It broke," he said.

"What?"

"The uhhh—"

Penney slammed her legs together, narrowly missing his belly. "What do you mean, 'it broke'?"

"Um," he said.

She came up on her elbows and looked.

"Fuck," she said.

The condom had basically disintegrated. The remnants of it coiled at the base of his penis, like it wanted to fit back into the wrapper.

"It's cool," he said. "I have another one."

Did no one else pay attention in health class? "Uh . . . nope." Penney squeezed her knees tighter and rolled toward the edge of the mattress. She hustled off to the bathroom, running water between her legs to scrub it out.

"Try again?" Colby asked, a fresh foil pouch in hand.

"The magic is gone," Penney informed him. "At least *you* got off."

"Was it okay?" he said. "I mean, was it good for you?" He looked so puppy-dog hopeful. She let out a little cough to cover her laugh.

"Uh, yeah, sure. Right up until the end there, you know?"

Mina

"Was it good for you?" Chip asked, racking the driver's seat upright.

"Yeah." Mina fumbled with the straps of her prom dress. "Second time's the charm."

Chip frowned slightly at her honesty. Whatever. She wasn't going to lie to protect his feelings. One out of two was good enough for her. Better than most girls got.

Mina plucked a couple of loose white sequins off her thighs, then tugged the short skirt of her dress back over her hips. She was still pleased with her selection of outfit. The tight cut hugged her curves, the white fabric accenting the smooth dark brown of her skin. Chip was admiring her appearance, she could tell by his stillness.

"So, you feel good?" He doubled down.

"You're hot, baby. You know that," Mina added, to soothe his ego. "Every time with you is a good time. No one's keeping score." She leaned over and kissed his neck.

It was too much work, always reassuring him. Three weeks to graduation. Come summer, she'd find a way to end things. Chip was all kinds of fun, the ideal senior year boyfriend—he had access to all the good parties and was ready for anything with muscles for days. No regrets. She could run her fingers through that floppy blond hair all day and night. But things were changing. She was headed to Kenyon in the fall, with Chip set to be a three-and-a-half-hour drive away at Ball State. Two hundred miles. He'd mapped it the other night, talking about going back and forth weekends. She hadn't had the heart to nip it in the bud in the moment, but there was no way she was going to college with boyfriend baggage on the roof rack.

For now, though, it was fine. Better than fine. Chip drove with one hand on the wheel and the other under her skirt. Captain of the football team meant serious competitive spirit. Can't leave the field without going for the touchdown. One Hail Mary to even the score. Mina closed her eyes and went along for the ride, gripping the seat belt when he finally found the place that made her squirm. Ideal senior year boyfriend.

"Better?" Chip said, parking at the curb in front of her house.

Mina grinned. "I said it was good to begin with." She kissed him, then collected her purse and her panties out of the footwell.

"You wanna chill tomorrow?" he asked.

"I wanna sleep tomorrow," she answered. "See you Monday?"

"Monday," he said, kissing her again.

Mina pulled away, after a time. It always felt so good, and she was always the one to pull away. Always would be, she understood. She'd come to rely on his arms cupping her. Someone to give her a ride and someone to press her hand into. It might be easier, she supposed, to keep it going. To not let anything change. But she had to. Because Chip might always be here, but she was going places.

Chip stroked her cheek. "I love you."

"I love you too." It wasn't a lie, exactly. Love was more complicated than simple, Mina knew now. The attraction part, that was simple. Looking into his eyes, not so much.

Sheryl

It didn't have to happen.

The words pounded through Sheryl's brain like a drumbeat. *It didn't. Have. To Happen.*

She sat on the bathroom floor through the wee hours of the night, contemplating the handful of problems ahead of her. She leaned against the sink cabinet and ran her fingers along the ceramic lip of the bathtub. All she wanted was a shower. But it had been drilled into her for years—if any man ever lays a hand on you, report it. Let alone if he . . .

It didn't have to happen.

The moments replayed in her mind. Fast motion. Slow motion. Forward. Backward. The points where she should have left, the points where if one tiny thing had gone differently, maybe everything would have been different. The point where it was happening and she was stuck in it, helpless, inert.

It didn't have to happen.

The house phone sat on the pea-green bath mat beside her. She couldn't call the cops. No one wanted cops coming to the house. She'd lose this foster home for sure if she brought that much drama up in here.

It didn't have to happen.

Rob had always been a sweet guy, around campus. With a couple of drinks in him, he became another guy altogether. Sheryl hadn't seen that coming.

It didn't have to happen.

They'd been science lab partners all year in AP Bio. It was dumb alphabetical luck, because they had to sit in rows by last name and when it came time to choose lab partners—that's right, *choose*—there must have been an uneven number of cool kids in class, because Rob turned those radiant blue eyes on her and said, "Wanna do it?"

It didn't have to happen.

All the health class lessons and after-school specials in the world hadn't prepared her for the rush of blood to that private place between her legs. When he gazed into her eyes, she melted like a chocolate chip cookie.

There had been many moments between them since then. That's what she called them in her head. Moments. A brush of fingers against a pipette. Elbows bumping while they took notes, because he was right-handed and she was left, and neither of them ever suggested switching places. Sitting with their heads close together while pinning open the sides of the poor fetal pig. The formaldehyde smell was anything but romantic, and yet she looked forward to bio class extra that week, because it was lab day every day, unlike usual.

It didn't have to happen.

She'd flirted, no question. She'd smiled back. She'd leaned into his banter, let his hand brush her arm or his knee brush her thigh. She'd imagined him asking her out, never believing it would really and truly happen.

It didn't have to happen.

It never quite made sense to her, why he'd asked her to prom. Surely he had girlfriends, or at least many options. He was popular, though not Prom King popular. In other words: not so vapid and image conscious as some of the cool kids. More like smart-handsome-nerd popular. He had a table full of good-looking friends of all genders and was always talking about some party he had gone to over the weekend. He never seemed to want for company or for a good time. His life seemed to Sheryl to be a landscape of choices, between girls and cars and friends and colleges. His toughest choices in recent weeks involved deciding between Yale and Princeton and deciding whether he wanted a Mercedes or a Lexus for high school graduation, to upgrade from the Acura he'd gotten when he turned sixteen. He'd told her all about it over the fetal pig, and she'd tried her best to act like those dilemmas sounded totally normal and not wildly pie-in-the-sky. Sheryl's own grades were good enough to get into college, with options in and out of state, but the only place she could afford in the end was the one that had given her a full scholarship.

It didn't have to happen.

Sheryl stared up at the showerhead, craving the feeling of its power rushing over her. It was all she wanted. It was all there was, except, she was a practical sort of person. Or, she tried to be. She also tried to live with no regrets, unlike everyone around her, who seemed full of them.

She had watched enough *Law & Order* to know there was only this moment. The shower would be the beginning and the end of the no take backs.

The thought of looking at Rob's grinning face in AP Bio come Monday was ultimately too much to take.

She couldn't do it. She had to tell. And hopefully she would never have to see him again.

Her fingers fumbled over the bath mat and grasped the phone. She dialed the only phone number she still had memorized.

The phone rang seven times before a sleepy woman's voice

growled, "It's four in the morning, asshole. This had better be good."

"Tana?"

The woman's voice shifted. "Sheryl? That you, kitten?"

"Yeah."

"It's early, babe. What's wrong?"

Sheryl burst into tears.

"Hey. Hey. Talk to me." Tana sounded fully awake now. "What happened?"

"Can you come get me?"

"Where? Are you in trouble? Can you get to somewhere safe?"

Through the line, Sheryl heard rustling and thumping and keys rattling.

"I'm at the house." She rattled off her current address.

"And you're safe there? Do I need to call the police?"

"No. I just, um . . . I think I need you to drive me to the hospital."

Penney

Penney burst into the twenty-four-hour pharmacy like her tail was on fire. Sure felt like it was. She raced through the cold/allergies aisle and knocked a few nonprescription reading glasses off their rack as she rounded the corner at the end. She fumbled a moment, trying to pick them up, but their cords got tangled together and she was out of her mind, so she abandoned them in a heap on a random shelf beside a similarly abandoned pack of adult diapers.

She flopped against the prescription "drop off" counter and pounded the service bell with her fist.

A perky blond pharmacy tech emerged from within the shelves of medicine. "Can I help you?"

"The condom broke," Penney blurted out. The place was otherwise empty, and anyway, who cared if someone overheard? She had bigger problems tonight.

"I see."

"I heard there was this pill you could get," Penney said. "The morning-after pill?"

"Well, there is, but you need a prescription for that, hon," the tech said. "You have to call your doctor."

"No, I read that it was going to be available over the counter."

"Soon, maybe. It's still awaiting final FDA approval. They've been trying for a few years now and hitting roadblocks."

"No!" Penney moaned in despair. "I have to have it. Like, I HAVE to have it. You don't understand."

"I do, but I'm afraid . . ."

"Please! Is there anything you can do?"

"You can typically get the prescription if you're within three to five days of the intercourse," the tech said.

"I'm within five hours," Penney said.

The tech rummaged under the desk and came up with a business card. "If you can't reach your own doctor in the morning, the doctors at Planned Parenthood might be able to help too." The card contained the info for the nearest Planned Parenthood office.

"Okay." Penney breathed a huge sigh. "So it doesn't have to be the literal morning after? You have five days?"

"No, you want to take it as soon as possible," the tech corrected her. "Ideally within twenty-four hours."

"I can't get pregnant."

The tech smiled patiently. Perhaps it was not her first midnight rodeo. "Pregnancy doesn't occur instantly," she explained. "The sperm and the egg are both very small. In order for fertilization to happen, the egg has to be present and the sperm has to have time to find it. So, both the egg and the sperm will spend several days in the body, hoping for a match. Biologically speaking."

Penney's stomach lurched. "I'm sorry, what?"

"There are several conditions that have to be met for pregnancy to happen. During ovulation, the ovary deposits an egg into the fallopian tube. After ejaculation, the sperm make their way through the uterus to the fallopian tubes, looking for the egg."

Penney was horrified. "They're STILL IN ME? Like, waiting?"

The tech nodded. "Plan B primarily works by preventing ovulation for a few days, ideally allowing the sperm to live out its timeline without finding an egg."

"Okay." Penney tried to calm herself with a deep breath. She would call the doctor first thing in the morning.

"Even if fertilization does occur, the fertilized egg still has to move out of the fallopian tube and implant itself in the uterus. Plan B hormones can sometimes prevent the fertilized egg from implanting successfully."

"So there's hope?"

"Certainly, though of course I can't guarantee any particular outcome." The tech paused. "Where are you in your cycle, hon?"

"Um . . ."

"When was your last period?"

"First of the month," Penney said. "It's usually around then."

"Pretty regular cycle?" the tech asked.

"Like clockwork."

The tech nodded. "Well, it's hard to say for sure, because everybody is different. But ovulation happens mid-cycle, about halfway between the start of two adjacent periods. So you're going to want that prescription as soon as possible, hon."

"Because I had my period over two weeks ago." Penney felt a sinking sensation in her stomach. Now she understood. "And if I've already ovulated, it might be too late."

Sheryl

The shower. Finally.

The indignity of the rape kit had activated the rage in every cell of her being. She was hot with it. She ran the water even hotter.

When the officers had asked her, did she know the man who had raped her, she said it loud and clear.

"Rob Clayton. My prom date."

The officers glanced at each other. "Would that be Robert Clayton the third, son of Rob Clayton, Jr., the defense attorney?"

"Um, I don't know. His dad's a lawyer, I think." She rubbed her forehead. "I don't know his name for sure."

"You don't know your rapist's name for sure?"

"I don't know his dad's name. Why would I know his dad's name?" Sheryl said. "I already told you, I know who . . . it was Rob Clayton."

"Rob Clayton is a powerful man in the community, miss," said one of the officers. "You don't know him?"

Sheryl stared at them. "No."

Their eyes on her. The harshness of their voices. The way they kept repeating Rob's name and talking about his father, the big-time lawyer.

She wanted to wash that off too. And the sinking feeling in her gut that her words hadn't been enough.

"Did you fight?" they'd asked.

"I—I tried to push him off at first."

"Scratch, claw, kick?"

"No," Sheryl whispered. "I just wanted it to be over." Was that her mistake? If she'd fought him off harder, might it not have happened? She remembered feeling frozen, as though her limbs were too heavy to move.

"So, you let him have sex with you, and later changed your mind?"

"No," Sheryl said. She tried to sound firm, but her voice wavered.

"If you didn't fight him, there's not going to be much evidence of rape."

She hadn't known what to say to that. Her stomach sank into oblivion. She'd touched the scratch on her neck where his hand had pressed her into the mattress.

Now she touched it again, sticking her head under the flowing water. Despite the soothing heat of the shower, it was hard to erase their cold tone of voice from her memory.

"You went to the hotel with him voluntarily?"

"He drove there without asking me."

"But you went inside. Did you ask him to take you home instead?"

"Not at that point, no. He had been nice. He said he had prepared the room for us. It seemed rude. I didn't know he was going to—"

"So you didn't think going into a hotel room with your prom date signified anything?"

Sheryl thought for a moment. "No?" Looking back, it seemed obvious, what he might have been expecting. But at the time it had seemed innocent. He'd been so nice. They'd been having fun. She'd been looking forward to a little make-out session in a comfortable place.

How could she have known he'd try to ply her with alcohol? That he'd get mad when she refused it? That he'd say she owed him. That he'd pin her down and—

She shuddered.

The water steamed on, hot and long. It couldn't be hot enough. It wouldn't be long enough. So finally, she turned it off.

Tana had the kindness to bring her a fresh set of clothes. Sheryl didn't know how or where they came from, but the yoga pants were soft navy blue and the sweatshirt felt like butter in her hands. They weren't from some neighborhood discount store, that much was for sure.

She wiped a layer of fog off the mirror with her fist. She studied her reflection as she combed her hair with the plastic comb in the bag from Tana. Too bad she hadn't looked like this when the officers came in—all scrubbed and fresh-looking in quality threads, instead of in the pathetic hospital gown with makeup still caked and smeared and hair all a-jumble. They had looked at her like she was as dirty as she felt. Like she might never be clean again. Like she wasn't worthy of more than what she'd got.

And maybe she wasn't. Her skin stung from the heat of the water and the memory of his touch. Maybe it was the best she deserved. But she looked okay now, on the outside. And that wasn't nothing.

Mina

Mina slept in late. She woke to the smell of waffles and bacon. Dad's Sunday specialties.

She rolled out of bed in her PJs and jammed her feet into her fuzzy gray slippers. *Brunch, here I come.* This was shaping up to be a perfect weekend.

Her mother was seated in her robe at the kitchen table with the newspaper open and a mug of coffee warming her hands. Her father moved between the stove and the kitchen island, alternately flipping bacon slices and pouring batter into the waffle iron. Mom was the weekday cook, but Dad stepped up on the weekends after church. Sunday meals had always been a big thing in his Southern Black family. Mina's grandparents' Sunday brunch in North Carolina was practically a community event. Dad's three-person version paled in comparison, but it was still pretty great as far as Mina was concerned.

"How was it?" her mother asked, sipping her coffee. Her mother was white and half Jewish, so the concept of post-church brunch held less sentimental value to her, as did the concept of church in general. She was content to sit and peruse the Sunday paper and benefit from the bounty of brunch that would appear in front of her.

"It was great." Mina flopped onto one of the kitchen island stools. She regarded her mother's casual attire. "Didn't you go to church?"

"I used a get-out-of-jail-free card." Her mother smiled.

"Twinsies!" Mina exclaimed. That was what they called getting a pass from Dad to skip church for a week. Barring actual documentable illness, Mina was literally allowed three skips a year: one per school semester and one over the summer. She'd used her spring semester one this morning to recover from the late night after prom, and it was totally worth it. Being a grown woman, Mom technically could do whatever she wanted, but she followed the rules Dad had set out for Mina because the routine of church attendance was so important to Dad.

"So, how was it?" her mother asked again. "Did you have a good time?"

"Yeah, it was great." Mina knew her mother was hoping for more details.

"And your date? What is it, again? Chuck?" For the life of him, Dad couldn't remember Chip's name. At this point Mina was convinced he was resisting on purpose. He was a pretty smart guy who paid close attention to Mina's every move.

"Chip," Mina's mother corrected, with a weary tone that said she was onto his games too.

Chip? Like a chocolate chip? he'd said, back when Mina first mentioned him. *A white chocolate chip*, Mina had thought, but loyalty prevented her from making a joke at her sometimes-sort-of-boyfriend's expense.

"Right, Chip," Dad said now. "He was a gentleman?"

"A perfect gentleman, Dad," Mina assured him, grabbing a slice of cooling bacon from the paper-toweled plate.

"That comes out of your quota," Dad said, jabbing the air with the tongs.

"Don't worry, Dad." Mina kissed his cheek. "I won't infringe upon anyone else's bacon share."

"He treated you with respect?" Dad said. "Now, you know I'm a man of faith, but I will beat his ass."

Mina couldn't help but laugh. Her father was a practicing physician and pre-med studies professor at the local university. He was a large, imposing man, physically, and he could silence a room with one of his stern glares, but she was pretty sure he would be knocked over with a feather before he could bring himself to actually throw a punch. The man could fight with words and numbers, but only words and numbers.

"They don't make a spreadsheet for that," Mina quipped.

Her mother laughed. "Don't give him ideas."

"I'm waiting for an answer," Dad said, his tone unnecessarily sharp.

"What is the big deal, Dad?" Mina mumbled. What the hell was his problem?

"I'm responsible for you," he said. "I need to know that you are safe when you're out in the world."

"Ew, that's so antiquated," Mina complained. "I'm independent."

Her mother snorted. That was an understatement.

"Under this roof, you're under my care and you follow my rules," Dad said, pointing the tongs.

Mina didn't totally know where this attitude was coming from. Yeah, he was the authority type of parent, but it's not like she'd never been out on a date before.

She glanced at her mother, confused. Her mother motioned her over.

"Seeing you in your prom dress freaked your father out," Mom said. "You looked so grown-up. He isn't ready for you to be out in the world as a woman."

"You're my little girl," her dad said.

"Sure, Dad, whatever," she said. "You do know I'm going to college soon. Where I get to make my own rules."

Dad's chest puffed up proudly. "Third generation Kenyon admitted," he said for the thousandth time. "Soon to be third generation grad of Harvard med."

The familiar knot in Mina's chest tightened as he recited his new favorite phrases. He was so proud. She wanted him to be proud. Why was it also annoying?

"I have to actually go to college before I can get into med school, you realize."

Dad scoffed. "With grades like you get? With a father and grandmother who went there? You're a shoo-in."

"Nobody's a shoo-in at Harvard anymore, Dad," Mina reminded him. "It's not like it was in your day."

"That's why you have to keep working hard and keep those grades up," Dad said. He circled the island and kissed her forehead, offering her a second piece of bacon along the way. She accepted the bacon. His vision for her was a bit harder to swallow. He was so sure, but it wasn't a foregone conclusion. She'd have to bust her ass to keep up at the college level. She'd have to be in the top of her class. She wanted to make her parents proud. She wanted to follow through with the plan, but the thought of all the work ahead made her stomach so tight. She wanted to change the subject ASAP.

"Well, first I need to graduate high school," she said. "So how about I focus on that."

Dad frowned. "You're on track to be valedictorian," he said.

Mina sighed. Always, with the pressure. Yeah, she wanted to be first in her class, but it's not like she was the only smart kid in a class of four hundred. "That's not guaranteed, Dad. It depends on our final ranks at the end of the semester. I could end up third, fifth, or tenth. There are a lot of good students."

"Tenth? Nonsense," her dad said. "You're a shoo-in."

"Stop saying that," Mina groaned. She couldn't put her finger on why it made her so uncomfortable. He acted like her plans were a foregone conclusion. Like it would all just happen. Like she didn't have any actions to take or any choices to make. It didn't feel that way to her. At all.

"I'm just saying—" he started. Luckily the waffle timer dinged right then. Saved by the bell. Dad turned his attention to getting the new batch off the waffle maker.

Mina slid off the stool and pulled a plate out of the cabinet.

"Never mind. You're right, as usual, Daddy." She sidled up next to him and kissed his cheek. "Now, let's eat." She held out the plate. "Waffle me!"

Sheryl

Tana drove Sheryl back to her foster home. It was still mostly dark out, but the lights were on in the kitchen already. Sheryl glanced at the dashboard clock.

"Great," she murmured. "Now I have to explain why I'm coming in at six a.m."

"Want me to walk in with you?" Tana offered. "So she knows you weren't just out all night?"

Sheryl held up her wrist, still sporting the white barcoded hospital bracelet they'd slapped on her in the ER. "This is a pretty good alibi," she said. "And I'll already have to explain why one of her old party dresses is now sealed in an evidence bag. So I'm just going to tell her what happened."

Tana seemed surprised. "You feel okay about telling her?"

"I'm not embarrassed," Sheryl lied. "It wasn't my fault." She said it out loud. Intellectually, she knew it to be true. But her mind still scrolled through all the possible things she could have done differently. What if the cops were right? She shouldn't have gone into the hotel room. She should have fought him off harder. She should have asked him to drive her home immediately. She should have been louder with her No.

"Well, okay," Tana said.

"The only thing I don't feel okay about is seeing him again."

"Seeing him?" Tana echoed. "No, you absolutely shouldn't see him. Why would you try to see him, honey?"

"He's my bio lab partner," Sheryl said. "I'll have to see him tomorrow at school."

"Oh. School. God, I hadn't even thought about that." Tana's face folded thoughtfully as she took a moment to recalibrate her expectations from the adult dating world that she occupied. "Is that the only class you have with him?"

"Yeah." Sheryl leaned against the headrest, exhausted.

"I'll write you a note and get you out of bio for this week," Tana said.

What if I see him in the hallway? The cafeteria? What if he seeks me out? Sheryl flinched at the thought of him popping up beside her in the hallway, all smiles and energy, acting the fool like nothing had happened. Tears leaked out the corners of her eyes.

Tana looked Sheryl's battered self over. "On second thought, maybe you should stay home a few days. Get some rest."

"I can't miss school."

"We'll say you're sick. Tomorrow I can go pick up your assignments, anything you need from your locker. It's reasonable to take a few days to recover after a trauma, babe."

"I guess."

"If it had been a car accident, no one would think anything of it."

"I wish it had been a car accident," Sheryl whispered. She had been cut before, and healed. She'd even had a broken arm once, and healed. This, she didn't know how to heal from.

Tana brushed a lock of Sheryl's hair back. "You did the hard part for now. You filed the initial police report. Your complaint is on the record. That's huge. Now you can take a few days to think about it, if you want. The most important thing to do immediately was the rape kit. And you were so brave."

To Sheryl that didn't feel like the hard part. It felt like the hard part was only beginning. But she opened the car door anyway. "Thanks, Tana. I really appreciate this."

"Anytime, kiddo." She paused. "Well, that sounds bad. Hopefully never again."

Sheryl shuddered at the thought. She forced a smile. "I know what you meant. Thanks again." She shut the door and headed into the house.

NOW
March 2024

*"Patriarchal heteronormativity is so over.
I won't stand for it. Is this the hill I want to die on?
No. I want to level that shiz and keep walking."*

—Amber Harris-Rutledge

*"They say 'when you're ready, you'll know.' But I've heard
lots of people also say 'I thought I was ready, but I wasn't.'
It's all really confusing. If I think I'm ready—if
I know I am—could I still be wrong?"*

—Blossom Morgan

*"How do you deal when your whole life
turns out to have been a lie?"*

—Cole Brewster

Amber

"I can't believe we're caving to this heteronormative bullship." Amber craned her neck to see how many people were still in the prom tickets line ahead of them. It felt endless.

"You can say the actual curse word, you know," Carmen teased her with a laugh. "We're practically adults."

Amber shrugged. "It's more fun not to." She looped her arms as far as she could around Carmen's waist. "You really grew up dreaming of going to prom?"

"Not everyone knew they were queer back in preschool like you," Carmen said. "I grew up dreaming of being a princess. This is the closest option."

"Thank god you didn't run for homecoming queen."

"With this ass?" Carmen shook her generous booty. "I don't even think they'd give a ballot to anyone over a size eight."

Amber leaned her head on Carmen's shoulder. "When you dreamed of being a princess, did you dream of being a *thin* princess?"

"Unfortunately."

"Lucky for you, I like my princesses fat."

"Ha. Lucky for you, you mean."

Amber laughed. "Touché."

"Plus, it only stays heteronormative if none of the queer kids show up."

Amber tipped her head thoughtfully. "Not sure that's true. Prom's built on a really gendered concept."

"It's also a dance. The only dance left before we graduate."

They stepped forward as the line moved. Only one couple ahead of them now. The prom ticket table was festooned with streamers and small balloons. If that was any indication of how the ballroom would be decorated on prom night, Amber had questions.

Sighing, Amber rested her cheek on Carmen's shoulder. "Then let's make the most of it, right?"

"Thank you." Carmen kissed her forehead. Amber tipped her face up for a proper smooch.

"Get a room," said the random guy behind them in line.

"Get a life," Amber shot back.

"You know—" the guy started a retort, but his prom date elbowed him, then rolled her eyes and continued studying her manicure. The guy sighed and gazed off into the middle distance, studiously ignoring the canoodling going on in front of him.

Several signs stood in plastic picture frames on the table. Amber peered over the back of the girl in front of her to read one.

COUGAR PRIDE!
Prom theme: "I was here." (Beyoncé)
Prom tickets: $75 per couple/$40 single ticket

Another said PROM RULES in big letters, with smaller print underneath. Amber's gaze flicked back to the first sign. "Eww. There's a markup if you buy your ticket single?"

"Gross," Carmen said. "What if you want to go with a group of friends?"

"That's gotta be unconstitutional, or something, doesn't it?"

"Not sure the high school prom committee cares about the Constitution."

Amber poked Carmen's bicep. "Hetero. Normative. Bull. Ship." Amber palmed her close-shaved head. "Just standing in this line is making me want to protest something."

"Shh." Carmen nudged her forward as the couple ahead of them moved out of the way. She and Amber stepped to the table.

Three sophomore cheerleaders sat behind the table in uniform. The letters emblazoned on their sweaters said *Jyssyca*, *Brii*, and *Abbe*. Apparently there had been a moment around fifteen or sixteen years ago when a swath of new parents developed an unusual relationship with vowels.

"Hiiii," they cooed, in unison.

"Hiiii," Carmen answered, dragging out the word the way they had.

Amber gritted her teeth, fashioning a smile and resisting the temptation to say *If there are three of you, you could be helping three people at once, instead of making people wait.*

"One couple ticket," Carmen said.

"We need to see your school ID," Jyssyca said, holding out her hand.

"Our IDs?" Amber echoed.

Jyssyca pursed her lips. "To confirm that you're students here. Outside guests have to be preapproved."

"You think we might not be students here?" Amber snorted. She glanced around the cafeteria. "'Cause there's a hotbed of non-students breaking in to enjoy all our delicious and heart-healthy school lunch options? Should I be covering this for the student newspaper? I've always said we needed a cafeteria crime beat."

"Must you?" Carmen muttered. Amber shot her a look. They both knew, God help her, that she must.

"You also have to be seniors," Brii chimed in primly. "At least one of you."

Carmen smiled placatingly at the trio.

"And we need you to sign here, that you've read and agree to the prom rules and dress code." Abbe tapped the third plastic frame with the tip of a manicured nail.

"Mmm-kay." Amber glanced at the page, picking up the pen.

PROM RULES:

—No alcohol or drugs permitted

—Buford High students only (guests must be preapproved)

—All students must follow the dress code (below)

BUFORD HIGH SCHOOL PROM DRESS CODE

YOUNG MEN

Tuxedo (black or other color)

—Tuxedos should include: bow tie or necktie, vest or cummerbund, dress shirt, jacket, and optional accessories such as suspenders or cuff links

—Shoes and matching socks (black or white/ivory)

YOUNG WOMEN

Formal evening gown (full-length)
Dressy cocktail dress (appropriate length)
Dress shoes or sandals

NOT PERMITTED

Jeans, cargos, sneakers, flip-flops, Crocs, ball caps,
athletic gear

NO ONE WILL BE ALLOWED ADMITTANCE IF
THEY DO NOT FOLLOW THE DRESS CODE.
Young women are required to submit a photo of
themselves in their chosen dress to the
main office for preapproval.

"What in the patriarchy?" Amber exclaimed.

Jyssyca folded her hands primly. "It's important to BHS that
we have a clean prom. That's what we all want, really, isn't it?"

"No sluts or hoes need apply?" Amber muttered. "Unreal."

Carmen kicked her foot. "It's fine. We understand."

"The hell we do," Amber bellowed. "Only the girls have to
have their outfits checked? What about the guys?"

Brii sighed. "The dress code for guys is more straightforward.
Suits and tuxes, obvs."

"Some guys do wear dresses, you know. And what about the
non-binary among us? Can you wear an unapproved dress if
you're enby?"

"Um . . ." Abbe glanced at Brii, uncertain.

"Other people are waiting," Jyssyca said. "Do you want the
tickets or not?"

"We take cash, card, or Venmo," Abbe added, tapping the QR code on the price frame.

"Cash," Carmen said, tossing seventy-five dollars onto the table.

Amber yanked her cell from her back pocket and snapped a pic of the rules. "This is so not over," she called as Carmen dragged her away.

Blossom

Blossom plucked an apple from the fruit basket and practiced her most casual tone. "Julio's coming over later."

"While I'm at this work dinner?" Her mother raised an eyebrow. "Should I allow that?"

Blossom crunched into the apple. "Why not? You like Julio. Probably more than me," she joked.

Mina kissed her daughter on the forehead and swatted her hip. "Only some days."

"Also, you can stop calling it a work dinner. We both know it's a date."

"It's dinner with a colleague, B," Mina insisted.

"I'm going to college in a few months. You can actually bring these guys home now, if you want to."

"I don't want to," Mina retorted. "You know I always keep it casual."

What Blossom knew was that her mom longed for a true love connection, but dating as a single mom had never been easy. There was an endless supply of men who were good for a few months of fun, and Blossom had long since stopped trying to get to know any of them.

"Mm-hmm," she said. "Someday you're going to sing a different tune." She hoped so, anyway. For her mom's sake.

"He's a colleague," Mina reiterated.

Blossom tilted her head. "Deception or denial? Who's to

say?" She sipped her Diet Coke. "Regardless, I think it's best if you don't sleep with him."

"Blossom!"

"What? You're always up in my business, being like 'Who's coming over? How late are you gonna be out?' What goes around comes around, mama bear."

"You're barely eighteen years old. I'm supposed to look out for you, that's my job."

"We look out for each other." Blossom tipped her head down and peered at her mother over the rim of her glasses. "Plus, you apparently get pregnant at the drop of a hat, so you're gonna wanna be careful with that."

Mina planted her face in her hands. "Clearly, I've created a monster."

Blossom laughed heartily.

Mina joined in, then added, "But that actually proves my point. How many times do you have to have sex to get pregnant?"

"Once," Blossom recited.

"And so before you do it, you will . . ."

"Mooooom."

"Blossoooom. Before you do it, you will . . ."

Blossom grumbled. "Make sure he knows how to put a condom on properly or do it myself like you taught me."

"Good." Mina kissed her daughter's forehead again, then sighed. "I was hoping I had another decade before you started bringing sexy Latin men up in the house."

"Ewww, Mom. Don't call him sexy."

"He's a good-looking young man," Mina complained. "What, I'm not supposed to have eyes?"

"Again, I say: ew." Blossom took another bite. "Not that you're wrong. He's fiery," she said. "But also really sweet."

Mina pretended to plug her ears. "La la la la. I don't want to hear it."

"Ew. Mom." Blossom noted the worried expression hiding under her mom's casual joking. She decided to put her mind at ease. "I'm not bringing him here for sex, okay? So chill."

"Make good choices," Mina said.

"Oh, my god, Mom. You're such a cliché."

"You know what was cliché, in my day?" She made a stern face and jabbed a finger in the air. "Parents who said 'No having sex under my roof, young lady. In fact, no sex anywhere, ever, for the rest of time.'"

Blossom chewed the apple. "Yeah, you're right. That's way more embarrassing. I'll take twenty-first-century parenting clichés any day."

"You make it sound like I'm from the Stone Age. Hello, I've lived most of my life in the twenty-first century as well."

"Maybe there's just way too much Grandma in you."

Mina dove across the counter, arms extended, tickle mode activated. "Oh, you take that back or I'm putting you in a chastity belt. I'll show you old-fashioned!"

Blossom squealed and scooted out of the way. "My brain is chastity belt enough for all of us, okay? I'm a total basket case."

"That's what I want to hear."

"Just keep your eye on the plan," Blossom said, kissing her mom's cheek.

"You're going off to college, and I'm going off to law school," Mina said. "No babies."

"No babies. Harvard, here we come." Blossom slapped the doorframe and sashayed through it.

Cole

Cole shoved open the door to his mom's office, shattering an unspoken barrier of privacy. The house was otherwise still.

It smelled like Mom in here—her favorite jasmine-lily perfume—plus a whiff of old, dusty papers. The office was half storage and half functional. By day, she did her graphic design freelance work at the desk by the window.

It wasn't like Mom had ever explicitly said "don't look in the filing cabinet." The whole office area was kind of off-limits, but also why would he care? Obviously 999 days out of 1,000 he didn't. Which unfortunately also meant he didn't know where anything was kept. So now he found himself sifting through stuffy mortgage papers and water/sewer bills and—damn, their family cell phone plan was expensive!—and cable bills and whatnot, looking for the tax paperwork that would answer the final question he needed for his scholarship application form. It was due by midnight, and he had a party to get to long before that, and hopefully it would last a little bit after.

Cole considered himself a live-in-the-moment kind of guy. Unfortunately, the college prep process didn't really allow for flying by the seat of your pants. It sucked. So much damn paperwork.

The idea of being in college didn't suck. Parties, new friends, new girls—more specifically, girls you hadn't known since grade school. Girls who'd never seen you with a face full of pimples. A garden ripe for the picking. He was looking forward to that, but the prep process was a literal nightmare. His mom wasn't rich, so college wasn't magically paid for. They'd always had what they needed and not a ton of excess, despite her only working part-time, and the FAFSA had come back saying they qualified for various loans but no flat-out scholarships, so he had been pounding the pavement. His mom said not to worry, that they had some savings and she wouldn't let him be saddled with massive loans that everyone in her own friend group was struggling out from under. He was going to state school, for sure, to keep the costs down. Probably Indiana because he'd heard they had the best party life, and that was what mattered most to him. Just like high school—as long as he kept his grades up high enough to satisfy his mom and not torpedo his future, he could do what he wanted in the balance.

He flipped through the file cabinet too quickly and didn't find what he was looking for. So he started again. Top drawer, then bottom. Systematic. Eventually he found it. The folder was large and jammed into the full drawer, so he tugged the whole thing out and stuck his sock foot as a placeholder in the spot where it had been. The files behind it, no longer pinned by the hefty one, flopped forward onto his ankle. He ignored them as he copied down the necessary numbers on a Post-it Note so he could enter them into the online application back up in his room. Great. That would be done. One less headache of paperwork on his to-do list.

Cole stacked everything back as he found it and prepared to slide the chunky folder back into place. As he removed his foot to push it in, he noticed a file in the very back of the drawer, previously hidden by a set of empty dividers. It contained a long white envelope with the words *Cole Settlement* written on the top.

Cole hesitated for all of two seconds. It had his name on it, after all.

The envelope was mostly empty. There was one small key on a Copenhagen keychain. That seemed random. *Who the heck had been to Copenhagen?* he wondered. His mom had never been to Europe, that he knew of. The key looked like a lockbox key or safe-deposit key. His mom had a post office box for her business with a key that looked a lot like this one. The only other item in the envelope was a check stub, the kind typically issued by a business or institution. There was a perforation at the bottom of the stub where the check itself had been torn off, and presumably deposited.

There was no amount on the stub, just several empty columns on watermarked paper. The only typing was at the very top, a check number (44603), a date (Jan. 7, 2024) and a name: Robert Clayton III, Attorney at Law.

A small, quick-looking handwritten scrawl across the check stub read:

He's 18. So that's it, then.
RJC

Cole felt a tiny stab through his chest. *He's 18.* Cole had turned eighteen in January. January 7, to be precise. The folder had his name on it . . . There was only one logical conclusion . . .

Weird. So weird, in fact, it couldn't be right. His mom had told him she never knew his father's name. They met at a college party, danced, one thing led to another. She'd been in high school, only visiting colleges. Anonymous hot teen sex, apparently, which was super gross to imagine your mom doing, so that was the point in the story where young Cole had always put his fingers in his ears. She'd tried to find the guy, to let him know, but had barely known where to begin. Whenever Cole had asked about his father as a child, the story had been the same. Of course, when he was very little, his mom's version of it had been a little more fairy-tale. *I only met him once, but we had such a nice time meeting each other that we made a baby that very night.* He'd had to put the rest of the pieces together as he grew. Now he understood that he'd been the product of a casual one-night stand.

There was a time a few years ago when Cole had been particularly angry with his mom for not knowing. For depriving him of a dad. That was how he saw it at thirteen, when his body was changing and there were things he wanted to know and wanted to talk about that he couldn't bring up in a house full of women. He had figured most of those things out now, but it still ached, the fact that half of his origin was this mystery, this blank space.

Over a year ago, Cole had secretly submitted his DNA to one of those online analyst sites, hoping some genealogy information would turn up, but nothing had returned about his father's actual identity.

He had also never understood how his mom could sleep with someone she didn't even know, until recently. Until he started hooking up with girls. At that point he started to forgive her, because it made sense to him. Why not get whatever you could when you could, even if you didn't know the person's name? Of course you would get drunk at a party and go for it with a rando. This school year, he'd slept with eight girls from his own school, girls whose names he totally knew at the time, by the way, but now the list was fuzzy. Tonight, hopefully it'd be nine. Which reminded him, he had to get a move on.

Cole slid the envelope back into the drawer, and as he headed upstairs, he made a note to ask his mother about the name

Robert Clayton III. There had to be some other explanation, right?

He pounded his way back to his bedroom.

There HAD to be some other explanation . . . for a check written to his mom on his birthday, proclaiming "He's 18."

He logged into his laptop and typed the essential numbers into the scholarship application. Reviewed the form to be sure he'd completed all the fields. Clicked send.

There had to be some other explanation for a secret safe-deposit box key and a hidden folder labeled *Cole Settlement*. Right? RIGHT?

He pulled up a new browser window and searched the name *Robert Clayton III, Attorney at Law, Indiana*. A fancy-looking law firm website came up. A local firm.

Some other explanation for an attorney living right here in town sending Mom a check? Maybe she'd used an attorney to try to find his father at some point. Maybe she'd overpaid and he was reimbursing her. Maybe he'd found Cole's father very recently, gotten some child support, and his mom just didn't know how to tell him. The check had only come in a month ago. Things had been nuts, between SAT prep and the scholarships. Maybe she hadn't wanted to spring the news on him in a vulnerable time. That seemed plausible. She was always trying to protect him in one way or another. It was annoying sometimes.

Cole clicked through the law firm website menu: *About us > Attorneys > Partners*. Nope. *> Associates*. There he was. A smiling, suited, middle-aged man. Blue eyes, sandy blond hair. Good cheekbones. Sharp jaw. Squarish hairline with a little floop to the locks above the left forehead. The hint of a dimple on the right cheek.

Cole swallowed hard. It was like looking in an older, more distinguished mirror. He got up and carried the laptop into the bathroom. He stared at the picture and his own face side by side. Was it really as cut-and-dried as it seemed? Or was it wishful thinking?

Amber

Amber sat cross-legged on Carmen's living room floor. "Totally unconstitutional," she muttered, for the dozenth time. She pecked away at Carmen's laptop, an item Amber craved but didn't own herself. As a budding journalist, it was the great pain of her life to still have to share a computer with her parents. Next year, she'd have her own. The op-ed she was penning now decried the "horrible, gendered prom dress code regulations and the patriarchal, heteronormative, anti-feminist expectations they were both built on and designed to reinforce." Though true, maybe that last sentence was a little much, Amber thought. Rather than deleting, she simply pressed enter and sallied forth, trying out new phraseology.

Amber read aloud as she worked. "The dress code regulations are stated clearly in print, and yet the young men of the school are trusted to follow them while the young women of the school are not. This is worse than gender discrimination—it is a bald statement of distrust in female students that smacks of systemic bias. It also draws a harsh adherence to the gender binary, an unfortunate choice—"

"Draws a harsh adherence?" Carmen echoed.

Amber paused, nodded. "Okay, that sounds weird. How about 'It also adheres to the outdated, scientifically debunked notion of a gender binary, an unfortunate choice for an event intended to be inclusive of all students.'"

"Since when is prom intended be inclusive?" Carmen said. "In your view."

Amber chewed her lip. "Yeah. I'll change it to say '. . . an event that *should be* inclusive . . .'"

Carmen's mom bustled in with a plate of orange slices. "Snack time, chicas! Do you want some nachos? Quesadilla? Both? You want the chorizo, too? You look hungry."

Carmen smiled. "That's the glow of righteous indignation, Mami."

Amber glared at the screen, frozen in her state of rage.

"Ah, you need to be well-fed to fight the man. Both, it is. And I'm adding the chorizo." Carmen's mom eyeballed the four empty soft drink cans on the floor. "Not too much more Coke, though, mija, you need to drink water." She pointed at Amber. "You too."

Amber dragged her attention away from the article. "Of course, Mrs. Vallejo. Thank you."

Carmen's mom smiled. She stuck a finger in each of the Coke can holes, expertly scooping them up with one hand as she headed for the kitchen. "Amber, you keep standing up for yourself and my Carmen and girls everywhere. I'll keep cooking."

"It's a deal!" Amber called after her.

Carmen reached for an orange slice. "All girls everywhere, eh?"

"This is definitely bigger than BHS."

"Gender inequities? Ya think?"

"Well, I can't fix all of humanity in one fell swoop, but let's hope I can stop us from having to model our prom dresses for Mrs. Ratliff."

Carmen shrugged. "I was gonna wear a suit anyway."

Amber's eyes popped. "Ooh. That'll be hot."

"I know." Carmen grinned.

"Wait, does that mean you'll still have to get your outfit checked?"

"I don't know, right?" Carmen tapped her fingers on her knee. "I'd be following the boys' dress code more than the girls'. Sort of."

Amber growled and made a new paragraph. "Dress code reinforces an outdated gender binary," she muttered, clicking at the keys. "What do you mean, sort of?"

Carmen knelt beside her. "I'm thinking tux jacket over vest . . . and nothing else."

Amber's gaze dropped to Carmen's generous chest. "Showing off the girls?"

"You know it."

"With no shirt?" Amber teased. "How risqué."

"Only the boys' dress code says anything about shirts being required," Carmen said. "There are literally no provisions for a girl in a tux. And as long as I'm occupying a gray area, I'm gonna do it topless."

Amber laughed. "Now that's a picture I'm gonna carry for the rest of the month."

"Mrs. Ratliff would shit."

"God, I'd pay to see that. You, topless at prom with those glorious boobs rolling out? Damn. You'll ignite all the young lesbians."

"Especially if you join me." Carmen wiped her hand across the air as if beholding a sign. "Revised prom theme: Burlesque."

"I could have an 'appropriate' dress with a train that rips off or something."

Carmen scooted closer. "Tell me more. How short would it be underneath?" She placed a hand above Amber's knee. "Down to here? Or only to here?"

"Ooh, I like this game." Amber set the laptop aside and put her own hand on Carmen's shoulder, tracing an imaginary neckline. "How deep is that vest V?"

"All the way down, baby." Carmen leaned forward, catching Amber's waiting mouth with hers.

Amber pulled away, glancing at the door. "Your mom'll be coming back in, you know."

Carmen tugged her close again. "I think we're safe until we smell the chorizo."

Cole

The party was going well. The music was pumping. The illicit booze was flowing freely. Someone, probably Astin, had passed around a few prescription pills, and Cole had been lucky enough to score one. That wasn't usually his jam; he was more of a beer guy, on the average, but tonight he was willing to do pretty much anything to take the edge off. He knew it was a bad idea, but right now he didn't care. His head was already too messed up on its own.

It should have been good news, right? Knowing—well, probably knowing—who his dad really was after all these years. It meant everything he had dreamed of was possible now. To meet him. To know who he was, not just his name but as a person. To let his father know Cole existed, too.

Except, that was the rub. The check, the secret envelope, the handwritten note . . . all of that suggested that Robert Clayton III already knew Cole existed. Which meant his mother had been lying to him all his life.

Whatever. He drained the cup of beer in his hand and circled back toward the kitchen for more. Tonight was not about worrying. Tonight was about escaping.

It wasn't that hard to push the heavy thoughts out of his mind. He was already feeling light. And horny, watching the girls frolic and bounce. The difference between this party and the last was marked. Last time they'd all had to stay inside. It had been nothing but jeans and crop sweaters, whereas this time, tank tops and miniskirts ruled the night. Spring had sprung, so to speak. He rubbed a drop of beer from his lips and contemplated a row of bouncing behinds.

Cole's head buzzed pleasantly. He bobbed his head lightly at the edge of the dancing crowd, contemplating his options. His eye kept coming back to this girl Emmy. She wore a black miniskirt and black bra with a sheer gauzy black floral thing over it. He could have watched her all night. If he was braver, he'd go up and dance near her. Braver, or drunker. He chugged on his beer.

Astin ambled up beside him. "Go for the skirts."

"Hmm?" Cole's mind tried to swim upward from the murk to make sense of his friend's comment.

"You're figuring out your move, right?" Astin's drugged-out gaze moved over him, pupils dilated like two black holes.

Cole nodded.

"Trust me, it's a hell of a lot easier to get a girl to raise her skirt than to pull down her jeans." Astin licked his lips, brushed his hands against each other. "Thighs like a superhighway, bro. Just put your hand up and see how she reacts. If it goes good, then you're in, man."

"What?" Cole blinked through the fog. He tried to imagine sliding over there and grabbing someone. He didn't consciously set out to clock the skirts in the vicinity, but he did, and there were several. "Um, I'm not sure—"

"They love it," Astin assured him. "At worst, you get smacked in the face. Totally worth it."

Blossom

"Will they or won't they? The question of the century." Blossom tossed the remote control down onto her comforter. "Can't someone do something more exciting with a high school rom-com already?"

"What else is there, in a rom-com?" her boyfriend asked. Blossom's delightful melodrama was normal. The subject matter, less so.

"Julio Mendez, are you reducing all meaningful human interaction to"—Blossom lowered her voice dramatically—"the sex act?"

"I'm not. The world is." Julio calmly picked up the remote and switched off the after-school special of a teen romance that they'd been watching. "The dichotomy really means more than that, don't you think?"

"Come again?" Sometimes he spoke like he'd walked straight out of a college philosophy class. Julio was extra smart. He'd been accepted to New York University with a full academic scholarship. Blossom excelled in school too, and was headed to Harvard in the fall, but she was still in awe of how Julio's particular mind worked.

"It's not only will they or won't they hook up or have sex, right?" Julio explained. "It's will they get together, will they admit their feelings, will they put aside the nerves and fear of failure to say what they're thinking?"

Blossom face-planted into a pillow. "Oh, god. You're right. All rom-coms are a lie."

"Eighteen years old and already a genius." Julio squeezed the back of Blossom's jeans-clad thigh.

"Ha ha." Blossom rolled over, causing his hand to travel to the front of her leg, fingers in the crease of her hip with his thumb close to—She wriggled upright. "No, think about it. The deception goes deeper. They make out like there's an end to this bullship."

"But the truth is . . ."

"Relationships!" she cried. "It's not like you meet your perfect person, work out a few comedic kinks, and then live happily ever after."

"I suppose that's a bit simplistic, yeah."

"You're my perfect person and we're still stuck in this weirdness."

Julio's cheeks tinged. "You're my perfect person too. What weirdness?"

Like he didn't know. Blossom tossed up her hands. "Will they or won't they?"

"I thought we agreed we weren't ready." He was generous like that. Making it a *them* thing when it was clearly a *her* thing. The very sound of his voice made her want to jump his bones, but she couldn't. She loved him. She trusted him. She *wanted* him. But . . .

She covered her face. "No. I don't know. I don't want to talk about it."

Julio sighed. "Feels like we're talking about it."

Blossom rolled into him. "You can be in this room with me, all cuddled up, without thinking about having sex?"

Julio opened his mouth, then closed it. Finally he said, "This feels like a trick question."

"No, I'm really asking. You're not, like, thinking about it all the time?"

Julio shrugged. "No. We do a lot of stuff together. I can beat your ass in Mario Kart for an hour without thinking about your actual ass. Too much." He smiled sheepishly.

"My mom had sex in high school and ta-da, here I am." Blossom made jazz hands.

"We'd use protection," Julio said.

So did she, Blossom wanted to say, but who wants to think about their girlfriend's mom like that? It was bad enough that she had to think about it, why should Julio have to suffer?

"Can we drop it for now?"

"Sure." He flopped onto his back. "I don't want you to feel like I'm putting pressure on you. That's not what I meant."

"I know." She was the one who'd brought it up in the first place.

"For real. If we never have sex, I still love you, okay? I'm not all about that."

"Wanting it isn't anything to be ashamed of." Blossom rolled toward him again, lacing their fingers together. "In my heart, I really think I'm ready. I'm just scared."

"If the only thing you're scared about is getting pregnant, there are so many ways we'll be protected. Condom, obviously. You on the pill. You want to add in a diaphragm and spermicide on top of it? No problem. Plus there's the morning-after pill. If anything goes wrong, we can get that as a backup."

"Today. But what if they outlaw it by the time . . . ? And anyway, it's not a hundred percent effective." Blossom paid attention to that kind of information. "Even if all options were legal in Indiana, I don't think I'd be able to make a different choice than my mom did. And I'm so not ready to be a parent. I don't even know if I want to have kids, like, ever."

"Sure."

"I mean . . . maybe. But I don't know." Blossom shrugged.

"It's super weird to think about," Julio said.

"Right?"

Julio gazed at her thoughtfully. "So, is that really the only thing holding you back? It feels like there are a lot of options to protect us. Are you sure it's not—"

"None of them are a hundred percent!" Blossom steamrolled right over his attempt to shift the topic. "There's no universe in which you can add ninety-nine percent and ninety-nine percent and get better than ninety-nine percent."

Julio laughed. "Umm . . . That's not math. What you just said is not actual math."

"You know what I meant."

"I do know what you meant because the last time I was here you showed me spreadsheets. Don't get out the spreadsheets again," he hurriedly added.

Blossom frowned at him. She had looked up effectiveness rates for every kind of birth control they were considering. According to Planned Parenthood, condoms were 98 percent effective with perfect usage but 87 percent effective in reality, due to possible user error. Birth control pills: 97 percent and 93 percent. Diaphragms: 94 percent to 83 percent. The use of spermicide alone apparently got you 79 percent protection, and it added some extra protection when used with a condom.

No matter how hard she tried, Blossom could not convince herself that using a condom plus birth control truly lowered the odds enough.

Julio sighed. "All I'm saying is, there are a lot of reasons why it's a big step. Like emotional ones, you know?"

"No," Blossom declared. "We're good. We're good, right?" She gazed at him plaintively.

Julio took her face in his hands and kissed her gently. "We're great."

"Okay, then." Blossom sighed, relieved. The tightness in her body didn't entirely dissipate, but it basically never did. Having some level of anxiety was a forever problem.

"I always want to know what's going on in your mind. That's all," he said, hugging her to him. "We can talk about anything, right? Even when it's hard."

"Yeah." She leaned into him, but the moment of silence that followed felt full of unspoken things. She breathed in his scent and closed her eyes, feeling his heart beat strong beneath her cheek.

"Also, there are other ways," he reminded her. "We're talking about it like there's only one way to have sex, but we could do hand stuff. There are plenty of options that don't risk pregnancy."

Blossom glanced down at his fly. "Maybe."

Julio sighed. "Okay, not today, though. Today, we don't do anything."

"Anything?"

"Bloss, I heard a no, followed by like six maybes. So if we do anything today, I'm gonna feel like I pressured you into it. And that's not cool."

"Not even kissing?" Blossom frowned overdramatically.

"Kissing doesn't count."

"Now who's sending mixed signals, Mr. 'there's more than one way to have sex'?"

Julio laughed. "Kissing is okay, because we've already crossed that bridge. And we both know how we feel about it. I mean, no new bridges crossed."

"Life is a journey, not a destination, and all?"

"Don't knock the destination," Julio said, sliding his hand

over her hip. "I'm quite looking forward to the destination, but there are plenty of desirable tourist stops along the way." He nuzzled her collarbone. "Permission to explore the view from the twin peaks?"

Blossom drew her shoulders back, raising her breasts toward him. "Granted."

Cole

The hand trick had worked. Cole had pretended not to hear Amber's voice in his head saying *don't be such a dog,* and gone for it. What did he have to lose? It's not like he walked up to a total stranger and grabbed her out of nowhere. There was context.

This girl Emmy had been looking particularly hot tonight. Dancing, with her arms raised over her head, causing the crop top to ride up in that perfect way that showed off her impossibly flat belly. Flat, except for that little part under the top of her skirt that bulged out just a little bit. It was exactly the right size to palm while she was dancing, to press her backward against him while she was in mid-twirl.

She knew him, from English class freshman year. They might have had two or three classes together over the years, he thought.

"Hey, Cole," she'd cooed as he sidled up to her on the dance floor, trying to act like he was feeling the rhythm and not just wanting to feel her. "Dance floor" was generous to begin with. It was the patch of rug between the entry hall and the dining room of the house they were in, which happened to be where a cluster of people were grooving at the moment.

He'd laid his hand on her belly and pulled her toward him until her butt bumped against his crotch. They swayed for a second. She leaned forward a little, shooting him a startled glance over her shoulder. But she didn't twist away. So he held her close with one hand and let his other hand slide up her thigh.

Then she did twist away. "Someone's getting fresh," she said. "What are you doing, Cole?" She turned and put her hands on his shoulders.

"You're the hottest girl here. Gotta take my shot, right?" Cole felt dizzy, from her closeness, from the beers. He felt bold. Successful. He put his arms around her waist and pulled her close again, this time facing him.

She giggled. "You think I'm hot?"

He leaned in close to her ear. "Can't you tell?"

That was half an hour ago.

"I want you, baby," he said now, leaning up against her where she lay, reclined against the back seat of his Camry.

"I want you too," she breathed.

Cole reached forward and fumbled in the seat back pocket for the box he kept in there. He liberated one wrapped square as he leaned up and kissed Emmy again. God, she was hot. Her warmth beneath him, their bare stomachs pressed together, breathing hard in time to the soft radio music. Perfection.

He pressed the rubber circle to one side, out of the way, then ripped open the condom pack with his teeth.

"Whoa, hang on," Emmy said. "What are you doing?"

"I'm keeping you safe, baby. Safety first." His mom had gotten pregnant her senior year in high school, so he wasn't taking any chances. Shifting details aside, that much was still true, and it was still true that he had grown up fatherless, because the dude never called, never wrote, never showed up to own his actions. Cole wouldn't be like that. So the condom was essential for him in particular, above and beyond just being good sense. But now he was annoyed that Emmy had brought it up, because it forced him back into the train of thought he was desperately trying to avoid, the train of thought that led to Robert Clayton III, attorney at law, and all of his mother's lifelong lies.

"Shh," he assured Emmy. "I've got you."

"It's a little soon, don't you think?" Emmy said. The words floated at the back of his train of thought.

"Soon?" Cole echoed. "We've been here like an hour." He had never been harder in his life.

"But, like, we just . . . I don't really think . . ." Emmy's voice trailed off.

Cole's hand kept working. They wanted each other. What was to think about?

"Hang on," Emmy said. Her voice was a little bit breathless. He was doing a good job.

"One second," he said.

"Wait—"

"Yeah, just wait one second," he agreed.

"No, WAIT. Stop." Her hand pushed against his shoulder. The resistance helped him gain leverage.

"Yeah," he said. "That's good."

"Cole, I'm saying no."

"You know you love it," he murmured. Five seconds ago she was moaning in pleasure. She'd said, *I want you too.* Nobody could change gears that fast.

"Cole!" she shouted.

"What?" he panted.

"Don't be a jerk," she said. "I said, NO."

"No?" he echoed, confused.

"Get off of me." She pushed his shoulder. "Now."

Cole reached up and touched her damp cheeks. They were wet with sweat and the residue of kissing, but also the slim tracks of two tears.

"What's wrong?" he asked, scrambling off of her.

Emmy tucked herself into a ball, dragging her limbs out from under him. "I want to go home," she said.

"Oh," he said. "Okay. Sorry. I thought we were going to . . . you know."

"No," she said. "I didn't agree to that."

Your body sure seemed to agree, he thought. Cole rubbed his forehead, which, admittedly, felt a little foggy from the beer and the mystery pill. She wasn't making sense.

Emmy spoke again. "I'm sorry if I led you to believe the wrong thing," she said. "I'm the kind of person who needs to get to know you better before going further."

"Oh," he said. "Well, okay. That's okay."

She glared at him. "Yeah. I know it's okay."

Um, well, she was mad at him. That was coming through loud and clear now.

"We don't really know each other," Emmy said. "I would want to talk a lot more." The words tumbled out. She was babbling.

"If you stop and try to talk about it, the whole thing tends to get shut down," Cole complained.

Emmy's lips parted. "Uhhh . . . do you even hear how messed up that is?"

"What?"

Emmy looked out the window. "Just take me home, okay?"

"Yeah, okay. Sure." Cole stripped off the condom—what a waste.

They pulled their clothes on and moved to the front seat.

"Why are you so upset?" he asked.

"You scared me," she said. She still sat with her knees tucked up against her chest, pressed into the door. Small and far from him.

"I scared you?"

"You're really strong," she said. "You probably don't know what it feels like to be pinned down. To have your words not be enough."

"What are you talking about?"

"I said no like four times and I thought you were going to just—"

"What, like force myself onto you?" Cole shook his head. "I would never do that. You were totally into it, I thought."

"I was into it, up to a point," she said. "You weren't listening. I said no a lot of times and you didn't stop."

Cole was pretty sure she'd said no only once. "I did stop," he said. "I mean we didn't do it, right?"

Emmy looked out the window. "Yeah."

He drove in silence for a few minutes, thinking about what she had said. She liked the making out but wasn't ready for sex. Okay. He could be cool with that. Totally cool. She wanted to get to know each other better first. That sounded like fun. He liked her. A proper date would give them a chance to get to know each other, right? Maybe that was the next step.

Cole pulled into her driveway. Emmy gathered her purse and scrambled out of the car.

As she got out, he leaned toward the passenger side, looking up at her. "So, how about next weekend? Saturday?"

Emmy stared at him through the open car door for a moment. Then she slammed it without a word and hurried toward the house.

"Was that a no?" Cole muttered. He watched her dart up the driveway, code into the garage, and slip inside. She didn't look back or wave as the door slammed shut behind her.

Girls, man.

THEN
May 2005

Sheryl

Sheryl sat patiently in the police station waiting room. She'd been here an hour. It was at once boring and over-stimulating: her own total stillness coupled with the bright light, busy sounds, static hum of people doing something, anything but dealing with you.

Tana had gone up to the duty officer's desk more than once to check on the status of their request to see the detective in charge of Sheryl's case. Her attempts to make an appointment had been rebuffed and/or rescheduled a few times already. Weeks were passing. It had been almost two months since the incident, as she now thought of it.

Sheryl wasn't surprised. The police who'd questioned her on prom night had made clear they didn't buy her story. Why would their colleagues feel any differently?

Tana, however, was growing impatient. She sat down with a thump. "It doesn't seem like they're even here," she said. "This is ridiculous."

Tana rummaged in her purse for a pack of mints. She had given up smoking years ago, but she'd confided in Sheryl that the craving still hit when she was frustrated or out of sorts. She dug through her generous bag with intensity now, displacing a handful of tissues, some lip gloss, a tampon, and her car keys in the quest for the roll of LIFE SAVERS she always kept on hand. *They're called LIFE SAVERS for a reason,* she'd quipped once.

Sheryl had been eight when they met, nearly ten years ago. Back then, Tana had been working as a child advocate part-time while finishing law school. She was the person who sat with Sheryl in every scary grown-up meeting for the next few years. Tana helped her talk to social workers and police, lawyers and new foster parents. They colored together while Sheryl talked to therapists and evaluators. They got ice cream after the often-awkward supervised visits with her mother.

Tana had been a true life saver in those days, offering comfort and consistency in the midst of all the changing foster homes and scary court appearances and back-and-forth with her mother. They had bonded. When Tana left that job for the law firm where she now worked, she'd given Sheryl her personal card. "Anything you need," she'd said.

Sheryl was assigned a new child advocate, and then another, and she soon realized that her connection with Tana had been very special. She began calling Tana whenever things went wrong. She remained a trusted mentor-sister-friend, and the only adult Sheryl knew for sure she could count on.

"We might have to try again tomorrow," Tana said now, popping a LIFE SAVER and stuffing the rest of the items back in the bag. She offered one to Sheryl, but Sheryl was no longer listening. Her attention was on the tampon Tana had unearthed.

It was nearly the end of the school year.

Two months since prom night.

Oh, no. Oh, crud.

"Tomorrow?" Tana repeated. "They have to come into the precinct at some point. If we come every day, they'll have to see us eventually."

Sheryl was stuck, frozen within the impossible math problem. She counted the weeks over and over again in her mind.

"Sheryl?" Tana sounded concerned.

"Can we stop by the drug store?" Sheryl said finally, the bubble of dread swelling within her.

"You feeling okay, babe?"

No, come to think of it. She hadn't been feeling that great. Tired and moody and unmotivated . . . everything you'd expect her to feel after what happened, right? RIGHT?

"Sheryl?" Tana touched her arm.

"Tana." Sheryl's eyes welled up. "I think I need a pregnancy test."

Mina

Mina stood at the desk in the Planned Parenthood office and made the follow-up appointment. Her mind was still reeling.

"You caught it very early," the doctor had said. "You have at least a month to decide what you want to do."

"I know what to do," Mina said.

"Do you have someone to come in with you, hon?" the receptionist asked now.

"No, just me," Mina said. "I don't want anyone to know."

The receptionist nodded in sympathy. "Unfortunately, you need someone along with you. They won't do the procedure unless they know someone is going to be with you afterward."

Mina drove home, contemplating. The buddy rule was annoying. She could handle it on her own. She was strong.

She had friends, of course, but when she went down the list in her mind, she couldn't imagine confessing to any of them that she had messed up on this level. Taylor? No way her secret would stay secret. Joan? Not unless she wanted an endless lecture on the sin of premarital sex and to get dragged to confession. Avery? Definitely the best choice of the three, but she was squeamish about medical stuff and also did not possess any degree of chill.

Mina was a leader. The others all looked up to her. Plus, they didn't ever dwell on very serious things for long. They were into hair and makeup and all the latest fashions, cute boys, celebrity blogs, and hemming their skirts to juuuuust long enough to pass the dress code. They talked about chemistry problem sets and English essays and the calorie count on the cafeteria lunches. They were fun, no doubt. There was no one she'd rather share a meal with or laugh with at a sleepover. But she couldn't picture one of them holding her hand while her feet were in stirrups.

Mina's eyes welled up anew. How was it possible she didn't have a friend close enough to count on in a true crisis? That knowledge was both upsetting and disappointing.

She couldn't tell Chip, obviously. They'd used a condom. Would he even believe her when she said he was the only guy she'd slept with? What if he accused her of cheating? Plus, Chip's Christian streak was a mile wide. She'd been to his church a few times on a Wednesday night for the youth revival. Mina could get down with some Christian pop tunes and an energetic teen-facing service, for fun, but when push came to shove, she was more comfortable in the staid Episcopal environment of her family church. The evangelical vibes and auditorium seating at The House of Salvation made her uncomfortable. At the end of each service, they inevitably made an altar call, and Chip would always whisper in her ear, "Are you ready to surrender your life to Jesus Christ?"

Um, no, dude. She was not in any mood to surrender. Episcopalians didn't believe you had to rush forward and fall down on the altar speaking in tongues to be touched by the hand of God, or to live a life of true faith, or even to be saved. It didn't work like that in her tradition.

So Chip coming with her to her termination appointment was not in the cards. He never had to know. If they ever went out again—which was a big if, after this drama—she'd pretend she was on her period and beg out of the physical stuff. And, frankly, if she was going to beg out of the physical stuff, there wasn't much point in seeing Chip again, anyway. That was most of what she liked about him. Hell of a time to realize it. She sighed.

That left one, and only one, option. When she was sick it was always her mother who had taken her to the doctor. It had felt weird today, being in there all alone anyway.

The appointment was sixteen days away. It took her ten of those to get up the nerve. She pulled her mother into her bedroom and confessed her sins. Her mother's eyes welled up. "Of course I will take you, sweetheart," she said, embracing Mina.

Mina herself was all out of tears. She leaned against her mother's shoulder. "I'm sorry," she whispered, the truth aching within her.

It had always been hard to admit mistakes to her parents. She vastly preferred to lie than confess. *No, I didn't break the vase. It must have been the wind . . . Crayon? On the walls? Maybe my cousins did it when they were here last week . . .* She wanted them to think her perfect. She wanted them to know she was a good girl, always.

Penney

The silence in the kitchen carried the weight of the world. Or at least the weight of a life, or two, or three. Penney's mother sat at the kitchen table. She lit a fresh cigarette, contemplating the news.

"Well, are you keeping it?"

"You kept me."

"Just 'cause I did doesn't mean you have to. It don't work like that. No one's judging, you hear?" Her mom puffed her cigarette. When she lowered her hand again, she fingered the edge of the place mat with her thumb and ring finger.

Penney leaned her hips against the sink. "All of this time, I never asked you."

Her mother gazed at her in silence for a while. Finally she said, "Is that a question?"

Penney stayed quiet. It was a question, and her mom knew it. It was a dozen questions, a hundred. *Why did you keep me? Did it ruin your life? Do you regret it? No matter what I choose, will you help me?*

"You gotta do what's right for you, kid. Ain't no one gotta live with it but you."

"I shouldn't be around all that smoke," Penney said. "Can you take it outside?"

Rhonda stubbed out the cigarette on the side of the sink. "You done decided, kiddo."

Sheryl

"How did it go?" Sheryl's foster mother asked when Tana dropped her off after the police station visit. "Any progress?"

"Not really," Sheryl admitted. "It doesn't seem like they've investigated the case at all. Tana was pretty mad about it, and she let them know."

Mrs. Jones pursed her lips. "Well, that may or may not help any."

"Yeah," Sheryl agreed. It was unclear if this was a scream-the-walls-down situation or a catch-more-flies-with-honey situation. She wanted to scream, but she felt completely inert, like she was moving in slow motion.

"At the police station I also realized I haven't gotten my period at all yet. So I took a pregnancy test, and it was positive."

"Oh, hon." Mrs. Jones opened her arms and Sheryl moved toward her. She felt like a shell, bereft, yet somehow she wasn't crushed by the woman's embrace. "That's not the news you needed, is it?"

"Yeah, definitely not." Sheryl let Mrs. Jones enfold her a moment longer. There was no comfort to be had, it turned out, and it almost hurt to pretend. So she pulled away.

"You need someone to take you to the clinic?" Mrs. Jones said.

"I think Tana will," Sheryl said. "I'll see when I can get an appointment."

Her foster mother touched Sheryl's cheek. "No one will judge you after what that Clayton kid put you through."

"I know."

"Look, I care about you, Sheryl." Mrs. Jones crossed her arms. "And I know that you're going off to college soon, but if you need a place to come back to, you're always welcome. For weekends, or a school break."

"Thanks," Sheryl said automatically.

"I know you been through a lot lately," Mrs. Jones added. "So if you don't go off to school right away, I don't want you to think I'd put you out in the cold."

Sheryl nodded.

"There's a program that will keep paying your subsidy after you turn eighteen, as long as you're a student somewhere," her foster mother said. "You can go on living here for a while with that, if you take a class in town. Without school, I'd have to charge some kind of rent, because it means I can't get another foster in. I hate like hell that it comes down to that."

"I understand," Sheryl said. She was surprised, in fact. Several of the homes she'd stayed in made it clear that foster kids got the boot on their eighteenth birthday. The nicest ones maybe let you stay over that night so you could sleep off the dinner and cake. She'd figured Mrs. Jones for that type because she knew how important the foster care subsidy was to her income.

Sheryl's eighteenth birthday would be rolling around in June. It was coming up soon, actually, but with all the stress and distractions of the last six weeks, she hadn't even begun to worry about it yet. She'd vaguely thought she could go stay with Tana for the summer before heading off to college, she supposed. But it wasn't a guarantee. She hadn't asked her.

"I don't know how long the legal case will take," Sheryl said. "It seems to be going slow. I might take you up on that, if I have to come back from school to deal with things related to the case."

"It's a racket," Mrs. Jones said. "You think you can trust those cops to stand up for you? Against a big-time lawyer's kid? Those guys are all on the same side, and it isn't yours."

"I know," Sheryl said. That was the overwhelming feeling she'd had this afternoon at the station. At least, before the newer, more overwhelming feeling had set in. The stick had turned blue. Holy God. It didn't even feel real yet.

Her foster mom shrugged. "Those police never do nothing."

"I guess," Sheryl said.

"Not for people like us. They wouldn't even give you the time of day if you didn't have your own fancy lawyer helping you."

"I know."

"She want you to press charges?"

"She said she'd support me, whatever I decide."

Mrs. Jones stroked her cheek thoughtfully. "Lawyers usually have money. A family like that."

"Yeah, they have money. He has nice clothes, a car."

"Thought so." Her foster mom shook her head. "You know, if you got a good case, they might offer you money. Maybe a thousand dollars, even."

"I don't know if it's a good case. The police aren't saying much, except to talk about how upstanding and important his dad is, and am I sure I want to do this." As if it was her choice to begin with. As if she was the one causing trouble by continuing to talk about it.

Mrs. Jones tilted her head. "If they're not telling you you don't have a case, then maybe you have one."

"Maybe." Sheryl shrugged. It's not like she could really trust the system, or anything the cops were telling her. Were they duty-bound to tell her the truth? Were they duty-bound to investigate her allegation to the fullest? Or would they sweep it under the rug?

"When they come, you should take the money. Trust me, hon. You don't want to be in the system going up against guys like that. They always win."

In her gut, Sheryl knew Mrs. Jones wasn't wrong. But she also wanted Rob to pay for what he had done to her.

Penney

Walking into the Planned Parenthood office wasn't supposed to be on Penney's to-do list for about the next decade. It didn't feel great. But, hey, the organization offered all kinds of women's health services. Not everyone who came there was pregnant, of course. Still, it felt like everyone she passed on the way in looked at her like they *knew*. But that was silly. It's not like the only reason people went there was to . . . well, she didn't really want to think about that. Much as she hated to admit it, her mom was right. She'd already decided. And it sucked. It sucked hard.

Penney signed her name on the clipboard pages at the front desk, then flopped down in a chair to wait. She picked up a celebrity rag from the fanned pile on the coffee table and pretended to leaf through it. Out of the corner of her eye, she clocked the other people in the waiting room. One super pregnant woman, olive-skinned, much older, heavily blinged with rings and bracelets. A couple of white thirtysomething women who looked like they worked for a living. Waitresses or strippers or mechanics, or something. They both had that been-there-seen-that hard edge about them, like Rhonda, with lines already carved into the skin around their mouths. There was also a dark-skinned woman who could have been close to Penney's age, but the business-casual attire and name-brand purse said maybe early twenties.

No one she knew. That was a relief. Penney needed time to adjust to the new reality herself before having it blabbed all over the school. As if she didn't get enough grief already. Everyone would know in time, of course, but it was barely two weeks to the end of the school year.

Telling her mom had been awkward. There wasn't enough cigarette smoke in the world to hide the disappointment in Rhonda's expression.

Telling Colby was going to be much worse. So it could wait. Not for much longer, but at least until it was all confirmed with blood tests and the doctor's nod of certainty. Until then, there was a modicum of hope. A sliver of possibility that the second blue line had been a rogue agent. Never mind that the second test had confirmed it—the whole package could have been corrupt, planted by a foreign government to frighten all American teenage girls into never having sex ever again.

If she didn't have the baby, perhaps she too could work for an intelligence agency. She pictured herself clicking down European cobblestone streets in a trench coat and heels, through the fog, making chalk marks on a certain brick to communicate with her handler. The flash drive in her jacket pocket carried important information, and by delivering it, she'd be protecting the identities of covert agents all over Europe and—

"Penney?"

Penney snapped out of her spy fantasy interlude. She tossed down the magazine and approached the counter. "Here."

The receptionist handed her a square sticker. "Through this door, down the hall on the right," she said. "Make sure your name and date of birth is accurate, then affix this when you're done. All right, hon?"

"Sure."

The sticker said URINE SAMPLE in small block letters across the top. Penney's name and information were printed beneath it.

On a shelf in the bathroom sat a line of empty, lidded plastic sample cups. Penney grabbed one and dropped a few ounces of pee into it. Roughly 2.75 ounces, according to the gray lines stacked up the side of the cup. The cup was clean on the outside, but warm to the touch. Gross. She screwed the lid on tight and gripped it by the top as she carried it out to the little metal platform across the hall that said PLACE SAMPLES HERE. She suspected that this was only the first of many indignities she would endure in service of motherhood.

Motherhood. She shivered a little. The word had a weight to it that scared her. What her mom had done wasn't easy. That was clear. She hadn't gone out of her way to let Penney know it over the years, but it had been impossible to hide.

Penney swallowed hard and delivered the sample to the platform, sending it off with a last little wish that the home test had indeed been wrong.

She walked back out to the waiting room and nodded to the receptionist, who dipped her chin knowingly in response.

The waiting room demographics had changed slightly. The preggo and one of the working women had been called back, and there were two new couples in the waiting room. A moony-eyed couple, a youngish man and woman with fingers interlaced, leaning into each other with obvious affection. And a girl her own age, also holding hands with an older woman. But not romantically, more like she needed something to cling to. Mom and daughter, probably.

Penney recognized the clinger. Her name was Mira, or Mina, or something like that. They weren't friends, but Penney knew she was a senior, like Colby.

A nurse stepped out of the hallway behind Penney and called out, "Mina?"

Damn. Penney slid into a seat at the opposite side of the waiting room and held her hand up next to her face. It didn't matter, though. Mina was in her own world. Her mom dragged her up out of the chair and nudged her toward the nurse. She followed the physical directions as if automated. The nurse took her arm and led her through the door toward the exam rooms.

Well, that was a bullet dodged, for Penney. Mina hadn't even noticed her. Penney reached for a magazine again and tried to relax. Then the outside door opened, bringing someone new into the waiting room.

Double damn. Penney's heart sank all over again. Another girl she knew, for sure this time. Sheryl, from her econ class. And Sheryl definitely saw her too. They made eye contact as Sheryl scanned the room.

It was an awkward situation, at best, seeing someone from school. Hopefully *Fight Club* rules applied to Planned Parenthood. Penney certainly wasn't going to tell.

To her surprise, Sheryl beelined toward her, tossing herself into the chair right beside Penney's. "Hey. It's Penney, right?"

"Yeah. Hi, Sheryl." Double awkward. They stared sideways at each other for a moment.

Sheryl shrugged a little. "*Fight Club* rules?"

Penney grinned, relaxing considerably. "I was literally just thinking that. Like, word for word."

"Cool." Sheryl nibbled her ring fingernail. "This is so fucked up. I can't believe I'm here."

So much for thinking people came to PP for lots of reasons. Penney decided to play it vague a bit longer. "Yeah?"

Sheryl glanced at her. "Are you . . . ?" She glanced down at Penney's abdomen.

"Not sure yet," Penney said. "Here to confirm."

Sheryl nodded. "Me too."

"You always keep to yourself, you know, you seem real self-sufficient," Penney commented. "I didn't even know you had a boyfriend."

"I don't." Sheryl caught a good piece of nail in her teeth and ripped.

"Oh." Penney should have kept her mouth shut.

"It's complicated."

"Isn't it always?"

"I guess," she said. "I haven't really talked to anyone about it."

"You can talk to me, if you want to."

"No."

The awkwardness multiplied, but Penney kept talking as if that would fix it. "I only meant, since we're both here and stuff. If no one else understands, or whatever."

"It's cool. I didn't mean no, like no to YOU, I just can't really—" Sheryl waved her hands, as if to encircle all the unsayable things. "It was kind of a bad situation."

"I'm sorry." Penney ached thinking about it. Even not knowing the details, it hurt to imagine being in this situation and having regrets. Penney regretted the situation, sure, but accidents happen. She didn't regret her choices leading up to it. She didn't regret taking Colby between her legs; in fact, she had insisted on it. And they'd tried to be safe, not just on prom night but the weekend after and the one after that. In Penney's world there had been no morning-after agony, knowing she'd slept with the wrong guy or been rash about it. That must suck.

"You seem really nice."

The door to the exam rooms flew open. The girl named Mina came racing out from the back of the office. Her mom leaped up and followed her.

"That could be me in a minute," Sheryl said with a sigh. "Wait, doesn't she go to our school too?"

"Yeah."

"Geez, it's an epidemic."

Penney cracked a smile. Anyone who could roll with the punches of unexpected pregnancy was someone to be reckoned with.

"Sorry," Sheryl said. "I've always skewed toward gallows humor."

"Let me get your number," Penney said, pulling out her cell. "We can keep in touch."

"I don't have a cell," Sheryl admitted. "I can give you the house number where I'm staying." She listed off the number and Penney typed it in. "It's better to call back than to try to leave a message with anyone," Sheryl added. "I might never get it."

"Roger," Penney said. The way Sheryl had said 'the house number where I'm staying' already painted a picture. It wasn't all peaches and cream in Sheryl's world, it sounded like.

Sheryl cleared her throat. "Not to pry too much, but are you keeping yours? If you don't mind me asking."

Penney shrugged. "I'm still hoping I go in there and they tell me it was a false alarm."

Sheryl nodded. "Here's to the false alarm theory." She gazed at her hands folded in her lap.

Penney knew full well she'd dodged the question. "My mom had me at eighteen and I turned out okay," she said. "So, I guess that's something. What about you?" Turnabout was fair play.

"I doubt it," Sheryl said. "I don't have anything to offer."

A nurse emerged. "Penney?"

"Good luck," Sheryl said.

"Back at ya." Penney stuck out her fist and Sheryl bumped it. It felt good, that contact. Electric. Not flowers-and-candles-I'mma-jump-you electric, but nearly as powerful in the moment. One quick hit of you're-not-alone.

Mina

Mina and her mom sat in silence in the car in the parking lot for a long while.

"I don't know how to say this," her mother began.

"Just say it," Mina said. What barriers needed to be up between them after what her mother now knew about her?

"I want to be sure you understand my views on life and choice," her mother said.

"What are you talking about?" Mina knew perfectly well that her mother was staunchly pro-choice. There had been a moment in middle school when Mina had marched in, fresh from indoctrination by an anti-choice social studies lesson, and declared herself pro-life. Lord, the talking-to that followed. She would never forget it.

"I know we're a churchgoing family," Mom said. "But you also know that I'm half Jewish, from Grandpa Clark's side."

"Yeah, I know. He keeps sending me dreidels." Mina smiled. "Remember?"

Mom laughed. "I forgot about that. It's funny, because my household was pretty secular growing up. He's gotten more attached to his heritage as he's aged.

"We don't talk about it much," Mom continued, "because it was important to your dad that you be raised in the Episcopal tradition."

"You think?" Mina laughed. "Important to Dad" was an understatement.

"But I do think you should be aware that the conversations about abortion that you hear in this country, especially here in Indiana, are deeply tied to Christian understandings of conception. Jewish law is very clear that life begins at birth. There's no ambiguity in that for me."

Mina leaned against the headrest.

"My reason for saying it is just so that you know, there's no moral confusion here. Legally, and scientifically, even, the cells growing inside of you are not a human being. Only conservative Christian faith gives conception any significance. And that's not what we believe, as a family."

"I know," Mina said quietly. "I mean, I actually do know." Everything her mom said had felt true to her.

"Okay," Mom said.

"I can't explain it, Mom." Mina looked out the window. "I made the appointment in the first place because I thought I knew what was right." She shook her head. "But it's different now that it's real."

Penney

Penney sat on the exam table, her feet dangling as the nurse took her vitals.

"The condom broke," Penney said. "It happens, right?"

"Yes," the nurse said.

"My mom always said to be super careful. She always says she's extra fertile and she figured I would be too."

The nurse smiled noncommittally. "Your chart shows you have a prescription for birth control pills? Are you still taking those?"

"No. Not since I first tried them last year. They made me really sick," Penney said. "Too bad, right?"

The nurse nodded vaguely. "There are other options to explore," she said. "An IUD or an implant?"

"Well, yeah," Penney said. "I was supposed to come back and try something else, but it's a little late now. Unless you're about to tell me the home test was a false positive, in which case, load me up."

The nurse shook her head. "Nope. The urine test confirms that you're pregnant."

Penney wasn't surprised. It was what she expected. She didn't even react, apart from laying her head down on the crinkly paper and letting out a breath. "Yeah."

"So, now for your STI testing. We'll just need to draw a little blood," the nurse said.

"Colby's not that kind of guy." It was amusing, actually. "If you knew him, you'd see. It was all I could do to get him to do it with *me*, let alone anyone else. We're each other's first."

The nurse smiled. "It's a standard procedure, just to be sure."

Penney felt a surge of frustration. "I'm not lying. I get why STI testing is important, and if either of us had been with other people, it would make sense."

"Even so . . ."

"You mean, in case he lied to me?" Heat filled her chest.

The nurse nodded. "You can only ever be sure about your own history."

Penney made a face. "You don't know me. Or Colby. Why do you have to assume he's a liar?"

The nurse shifted uncomfortably. "What we do here is look out for women's health," she said finally. "STI testing is one way to check your health. Information is always useful."

"I don't think Colby's lying to me either." She was about to have a baby with him. Was she really supposed to start it off by not trusting him?

Penney shrugged. "Well, sure. Whatever. You can test me. As long as it's free."

The nurse pulled out a row of small blood vials. "We're a pay-what-you-can clinic."

"I can pay for the rest," Penney said. "But I'm not paying for that."

Colby was a good guy. He was faithful. If she'd had the chance to properly choose a father for her future children, she knew she couldn't have done better. Would she have even slept with him otherwise? Probably not.

"Colby's a good guy," she said out loud. "He wouldn't lie to me." The needle pricked her arm and she hated the pinch of doubt that came along with it. She took a deep breath. *Trust, but verify.*

"Are you ready to talk about your options?" the nurse asked. "Or would you like a little bit of time to process?"

"I don't need time," Penney said.

"It's our policy to go over the options with you," the nurse said. "So that you understand the various choices you can make."

"I meant, I don't really need to hear about the options," Penney said. The prophecy was written. The truth had been foretold. "I know what I have to do."

Mina

Mina had been alone for all of an hour when there was a knock at the door. She was contemplating whether or not to answer when her dad pushed open the door anyway. She could tell by his posture that her mother had told him already. Mina really wished she hadn't. She needed more time to think.

"I don't want to talk right now," Mina said.

"I don't care what you want," he said. "You're my child and you're going to listen to me."

Mina struggled to sit up. "Not feeling much like a child today, Dad. Can it wait?"

"I trust that you'll reconsider," he said, plowing ahead with his agenda.

"Mom already made me another appointment, Dad," Mina informed him. "Can we leave it at that?"

He had the same expression on his face he'd had when she failed her seventh-grade science class. A look of disappointment backed up by strong vibes of "you are not the daughter I raised."

"I understand that it's difficult," he said, though his tone suggested otherwise. "But you have to think about your future."

"What if I am?" Mina blurted out. "What if I *want* to keep the baby?"

The air between them cracked, like glass shattering. The facade of the perfect daughter. The hope of the next generation following all the prescribed footsteps.

"That is not acceptable," he said.

Frustration surged in Mina. "Not acceptable? Who are you to say?" It had been drilled into her for years and years now. A woman's right to choose. A *woman's*.

"I am your father."

"And I'm going to be a mother," she insisted. "So I guess I make my own rules now."

Dad glowered at her. "Not under this roof."

"Then I'd better find a different roof," Mina declared. That was rash. But this was what happened when he came at her, guns blazing. Her independent streak came charging out like a horse breaking free of the pasture.

Her father's face darkened. "If you expect our support, you *will* attend college and med school. Your mother and I are not raising a baby once you decide it is all too much."

Mina's lips parted in shock. "You think I would drop a baby on your doorstep and run off?"

He glanced coldly at Mina's overstuffed closet. "A baby is not the latest fashion accessory. You can't get bored with it and move on when the going gets tough and you run out of cute outfits. You have plans," he declared, his voice rising. "You are going to make something of yourself."

Mina shook with anger. Her mood rose from a simmer to a boil faster than she would have thought possible. Her resistance was about something more than the moment, but it was too overwhelming to contemplate. "Get out of my room," she said.

"It's my room," her father announced. "Everything in this house is mine. And don't you forget it." With that he stormed out, leaving Mina to mop up her heart, boiling over.

Sheryl

Tana picked Sheryl up from the clinic. When she shared the news that her pregnancy was confirmed, Tana drove them to a nearby coffee shop. They bought two hot chocolates with a mound of whipped cream on each and took them into the park across the street.

"How are you feeling?" Tana asked.

"Screwed," Sheryl said. In every possible sense of the word.

Tana sipped her cocoa. "I know it's early to talk about your choices," she said. "But I'm here for you whenever, if you want to talk about it."

"I don't know how much there is to talk about," Sheryl said. "I can't have a baby. I have nothing to offer a baby." She barely had a home, let alone a job or a way to support herself. She was going to college.

"You have a huge amount to offer," Tana said. "But there are practical considerations to think about, for sure."

They walked in a silent circle through the greenery. Sipping the foamy chocolate was oddly comforting, despite the added warmth of the late spring sunshine. Inside, Sheryl felt cold.

"When I was in law school, I got pregnant and had an abortion," Tana said. "I don't know if I ever told you that."

"You said something once that made me suspect," Sheryl said.

"It was a consensual event, in my case," Tana said. "A not-so-great boyfriend. Luckily, I had realized he was not so great by the time the issue came up. But I still didn't know what to do immediately."

Sheryl put a hand on her stomach. She was constantly aware of the area now. She had been ever since prom night. She wasn't sure if it was all in her head. "Did you feel like there was life inside you?" she asked.

"I knew there was a potential life inside me."

Sheryl cupped her cocoa to warm her fingers. "And now? Do you ever wonder what that child would have been like?"

"Of course. I wonder." Tana smiled wistfully. "When what would have been the due date rolls around, I always buy myself some flowers. Just a way to remember."

That was a little surprising to Sheryl. Tana was not at all the sentimental type. Her apartment was a pristine monument to letting things go. Zero unnecessary clutter, zero emotional mess. At least on the surface.

"Do you regret it?"

"No, never. It wasn't the right choice for me to have a baby back then. I think I would have been sad and miserable and not a great mom. No kid deserves that."

"But, you're Christian," Sheryl said.

"Look, no one is saying abortion isn't a hard thing. It's sad and difficult, and there's no perfect right or wrong choice. And, yeah, I had to wrestle with what it is I really believe about when life begins, and what the choice meant to me."

"So you don't believe life begins at conception?"

Tana shifted uncomfortably. "I don't really know. That feels like the kind of thing only God knows. Or the universe, or whatever you want to call the force that gives us life in the first place.

"What I believe is that the question of when life begins isn't the only important question. There is more than one consideration. Like, what that life would look like, and whether there would be suffering. In this world we can't always prioritize preserving every scrap of life. I buy cut flowers on the anniversary of my due date to remind myself of that. Sometimes we make choices that serve a greater purpose."

"That's not the same thing at all." Sheryl frowned.

"No, but it's a reminder. If we, as a people, truly prioritized the life of every single tiny organism above all, or even the life of every human being, the world would look a lot different. It puts the question of being 'pro-life' into perspective for me." Tana shrugged. "I don't expect other people to see it the same way, necessarily."

"I think I see what you mean," Sheryl said. "A scary thing about bringing a baby into the world, in my specific situation, is knowing that the world around me isn't going to do anything to make sure the baby survives and that we have what we need. I'd be entirely on my own."

"I know," Tana agreed.

Sheryl squeezed her hand into a fist, crushing the now-empty cocoa cup. "But I always swore to myself that I would never be the kind of mom who would throw their kid away." *Says the foster kid.* Sheryl's own mother had endless issues that had kept them apart for years.

"That's not what abortion is."

"I guess." Everything Sheryl had been through in the last five years was justification enough to not continue the cycle of parenthood. Did she even know how to be a good mom, since she hadn't had one herself? Her mother's betrayal was painful every day. Could she really allow herself to create a person, knowing the possibility existed of hurting them so deeply?

Tana took her hand. "You realize I'm not trying to talk you into it, right? The decision is yours alone."

"Okay."

"I'm just telling you my experience, because it's different than what you'll hear from a lot of people around here. We're pretty close to the heart of pro-life America. The billboards alone . . ."

"Tell me about it," Sheryl groaned. "'Your baby has a heartbeat' and all."

"Right." Tana drained the last of her cocoa.

"I'm not anti-choice," Sheryl said. "I don't think less of anybody for getting an abortion. Especially you."

"I know," Tana said.

Sheryl stroked her belly. It was already slightly convex, probably due to her love of pizza more than anything else. It was too early for her to be showing. "It's weird, now that it's not an abstract question. Now that it's happening inside my body. I don't know if I can do it."

Tana nodded. "I'm here for whatever you need."

"Even if I press charges against him?"

"Yes, of course." Tana hesitated. "I mean, it does change the dynamic of that situation, too, if you choose to keep his baby."

"*My* baby," Sheryl said. The surge of possessiveness that coursed through her frightened her.

"Yes," Tana spoke slowly. "But legally, both parents have rights."

"No," Sheryl said. "Not when he raped me."

Tana looked at the sky. "Oh, Sheryl. I wish it were that simple. Unless he's actually convicted in court, it would take a lot for the state to let him out of his parental obligations."

Sheryl swallowed hard. "You mean, he'd still be considered the father?"

Tana nodded. "That's part of what you need to factor into your decision."

Sheryl didn't know what to do with this new information. She tossed her cup into a trash bin, then covered her face with her hands.

"Here's the thing. I know this family a bit," Tana explained. "I can almost guarantee that if you keep pressing the court case, they'll eventually offer to settle with you financially. But first you have to make your decision about the pregnancy, on your own terms. I would absolutely not say anything about pregnancy to the police or Rob's lawyers until you've either had a procedure or you're in your second trimester, but if it gets to that point, a baby provides new leverage for us if we do decide to negotiate a settlement."

"That feels icky," Sheryl said.

"Honey, nothing you can possibly do here is icky in the slightest," Tana insisted. "What Rob did, that's the icky thing. All you're doing is making the best of the hand you've been dealt."

Penney

Penney was sitting, bored, halfway through government class when she saw a blur of a person go racing by. She was pretty sure the blur was Mina, the girl from the clinic. She looked upset.

Penney raised her hand. "Could I have a bathroom pass? Feminine moment." She said it loudly and made a face, and all the guys in the room groaned, including the teacher (though, he at least *tried* to suppress it).

"Very well, Ms. Rutledge," he said, handing her the large wooden stick on a loop.

"Thanks, you're the best," she declared, snatching it up and scooting out of the room. Maybe he noticed that she took her whole backpack and all her books with her; maybe he didn't.

Penney entered the bathroom to the sound of soft retching from one of the stalls. She leaned her hips up against one of the sinks and waited. But instead of Mina coming out, all Penney heard was tiny, racking sobs.

"Mina?" Penney said.

The other girl gasped. "Who's there?"

"Hi. It's Penney Rutledge. We don't really know each other. I came to see if you are all right."

Mina flushed the toilet and emerged. "Not really, but what do you care?" Her makeup was smudged. She looked a hot mess.

Penney pulled down a couple of paper towels and handed them to her. "Start with these, but I have some softer tissues in my bag." She flopped it onto the sink and began rummaging.

"What are you doing here?" Mina asked, patting at her smeared mascara.

Penney took a deep breath, ready to come clean. "Not to pry or anything, but I saw you at the clinic."

Mina looked panicked. "What?"

"I was at the clinic the other day too. For, you know, reasons . . ." Penney drew a little circle in the air in front of her belly. "So, I saw you there. You seemed upset."

"That's because it's goddamn upsetting." Mina's face crumpled. Penney patted her shoulder awkwardly, and before she knew it, Mina was sobbing in her arms.

"I couldn't do it," she cried. "Why couldn't I do it? I have plans," she wailed. "I can't have a baby. What is that even?"

Penney understood completely. "I know. Believe me."

They hugged for a long time, in the strange, tiled silence of the institutional bathroom.

"Look, if you ever want to talk about it, someplace else, we could," Penney suggested. "It's weird and lonely to feel this. To be facing this. So, maybe we could compare notes?"

"I'm not pro-life," Mina blurted out. She shook her head. "I mean, I'm pro–human life, in general, and stuff, but I believe in a woman's right to choose."

"I know what you meant," Penney said quietly. "The thing is, right to choose means right to *choose*. Not just the right to terminate. You get to decide. No one else."

Mina rubbed her forehead. "I can't go home still pregnant. My parents will disown me. I'm supposed to go to Kenyon, then Harvard med. Like my dad."

"Is that what you want? To go to Harvard med."

"It's what I've always wanted."

"You made a face when you said it." Penney mimicked Mina's pained expression. "Harvard med."

"No, I didn't."

Penney shrugged.

"If I made a face, it's because it's all a mess right now. But I have to work it out. I'm going to be a doctor."

Penney shrugged again. "Sounds like that would be a heck of a lot easier than having a baby."

"I stopped babysitting years ago. It's hellish." Mina dropped her face into her hands. "Oh, my god. It's going to be like babysitting twenty-four seven. My life is over."

"It's not too late," Penney reminded her.

"I said something about 'what if I want to keep the baby?' I didn't even really mean it, I was just saying . . . But my dad flipped out." She deepened her voice, imitating him. "'You're not bringing a newborn under this roof.'"

"He sounds like kind of a jerk."

"No, he's great." Mina rushed to defend him. "It's that feeling when they're like 'we're not mad, we're disappointed.'"

"'Flipped out' sounds mad."

Mina shook her head. "Never mind. Forget it. I don't even know why we're talking about this. What do you care?"

Penney put her hand over her own belly again. "I saw you at the clinic, remember. So . . . we have something in common . . . ?"

Mina stared at her for a moment, the pieces finally clicking. "You're—"

"Prom night," Penney said. "Perfect cliché."

"I can't go home still pregnant," Mina said. "They're going to kick me out."

"Probably not," Penney said. "But if they do, you can come stay with me until we figure out what to do with you."

"They said they would." Mina gnawed a cuticle.

"I don't think parents like yours really do that," Penney said. "Didn't you get a car when you turned sixteen and all that?"

"No." Mina rubbed her forehead. "They don't believe in 'spoiling' me. I tried to buy a used junker out of my saved allowance, and they wouldn't even let me do that. Safety ratings." She rolled her eyes.

Penney laughed lightly. "Okay, if they're worried about safety ratings on your first junker car, they're definitely not going to leave you out in the cold. That's some helicopter shit right there."

"If you'd seen my dad's face . . ."

"Look, I know we don't really know each other, but I meant it when I said you can come stay with me until they come to their senses."

"That's a lot to ask."

"You didn't ask. I offered."

"Well, thanks."

Penney nodded. It was an easy offer to make too. One look at those diamond earrings and she knew Mina was going to be just fine.

"We should be allies in this mess," Penney said. And she meant it. "Girls like us have to stick together."

NOW
March 2024

Amber

Amber's article was a huge hit. The school newspaper had published it on the front page, albeit below the fold. The feature on the basketball team making it to regional playoffs had to take precedent, of course. Sports-as-the-default-lead-headline was a bone Amber had to pick with the journalism team itself, but she could only fight one systemic battle at a time, and she had her hands full with this prom mess. Circulation of the paper was already up 10 percent by lunchtime, and Amber suspected it wasn't because of the basketball. That wasn't what was different, after all.

In fourth period, Amber received a note from the main office. She was being called to the assistant principal's office. The indomitable Mrs. Ratliff wanted to see her. *This ought to be interesting.*

Amber gathered her backpack and headed down to the office. The secretary accepted her pass and pointed her down the hall to Mrs. Ratliff's office. Amber already knew where it was. Not because she'd ever been called there, but just because she knew things. She was observant, as a reporter ought to be.

She pulled out her journalism class notebook and knocked on the half-open door.

"Come in," Mrs. Ratliff called.

Amber pushed the door open and entered. She wasn't sure whether to close it behind her or not, so she stood awkwardly with her hand on the knob for a moment.

"Yes?" Mrs. Ratliff said.

"Hi, I'm Amber Harris-Rutledge, a reporter with the *Buford Bee*. You wanted to speak with me?" She had her notebook set already, and she dug a pen out of her pocket now.

"Ah, yes." Mrs. Ratliff turned away from her computer and motioned Amber to take a seat in one of the two chairs facing the desk. "I understand you have some concerns about prom preparation. Specifically, the dress code?"

"Yes, I wrote a whole article about it." Amber plopped her backpack in the second chair. She could clearly see a copy of the article on Mrs. Ratliff's desk already, but she pulled her own copy out of the bag anyway.

Why was she acting like she didn't know what the article said, when she obviously did, or she wouldn't have asked to see Amber?

Whatever. Amber took a deep breath and plowed ahead. "It concerns me both as a student and a journalist that the administration is supporting a position that stands in opposition to students' free speech and expression."

"I believe in free speech," Mrs. Ratliff said snidely.

"Glad to hear it, but the prom dress code policy currently fails to reflect that belief. What can we do to rectify that?" Ohh, that sounded good. She was doing well. "I'd be glad to include your proposed changes in my next article."

Mrs. Ratliff pursed her lips. "Aren't you the same student who wrote multiple op-eds decrying students wearing Confederate flag merchandise?"

"Hate speech is not free speech. That's proven constitutional law."

"Representing states' rights isn't inherently hate speech."

Amber jotted that quote down. "And that was the reason you gave for not amending the student dress code at the time. Indiana wasn't even a Confederate state, by the way."

"I'm glad something from history class seems to have stuck."

Amber nodded. "You're keeping history alive and well with these dress codes, that's for sure."

"Our dress codes are in place for a reason, young lady. You can dress how you like on your free time, and you're free to ignore the dress code requirements if you choose not to attend the school's prom."

"So, you're basically punishing students for having attractive bodies?"

"We are maintaining standards of proper dress, which is anything but punitive."

"It feels punitive, to those of us who don't share your identical view of what is appropriate."

"Appropriateness is not an unreasonable standard to expect."

"But why should you—or any one individual, for that matter—be the sole arbiter of what is appropriate? How is that fair? My mother says . . ."

"Your mother?" Mrs. Ratliff adjusted the corner of her glasses. "Your mother, who got herself pregnant at eighteen?"

Amber was affronted. "'Got herself pregnant?' Sounds like someone needs a refresher in basic reproductive science. It's just as messed up to blame the way women dress for men behaving badly. If seeing a smidge of upper thigh causes a guy to lose his mind, is the problem really with what she was wearing?"

Mrs. Ratliff pressed her hands against the desk and stood up. "This conversation has gone on long enough. The rules are the rules. The dress code is the dress code. Come to prom or don't; it's up to you, but in the meantime, you need to stop riling up other students with your nonsense."

Amber stood up too. "My 'nonsense' being the way I choose to exercise my freedom of speech? I'm surprised that someone so quick to defend students representing 'states' rights' is so staunchly against people representing student rights." She tilted her head thoughtfully. "Maybe that'll be my next op-ed . . ."

"Freedom of speech does not mean freedom from consequences."

"Oh, I know," Amber said. "That's why you can get detention for wearing a low-cut shirt but not for wearing a Confederate flag. Some free speech comes with more consequences than others."

"Riling up students with anti-administration sentiments could also land you in detention."

"Well, there's a quote." Amber scribbled it in her notebook, word for word.

"Excuse me?"

"I write for the school paper," Amber reminded her. "You're on the record threatening me for writing my opinions about administration policy."

"Absolutely not. This is not an interview."

"I announced my credentials at the start of this conversation. You knew you were talking to a reporter."

"You're in trouble, young lady."

"You should ask for people's pronouns before you call them things like 'young lady.' I don't particularly aspire to be a lady. This isn't the Victorian era."

"You're walking a very thin line, miss."

"It's really the same with 'miss,' do you get what I'm saying? I happen to identify as female, but you never asked me. I could as easily be non-binary or trans. Gender is complicated, and it shouldn't be used as the basis for . . . really, for anything anymore."

Amber took a deep breath. Pushing it, pushing it. She had made her point and was dancing on the edge of discipline. Speaking truth to power was better left for the pages of the newspaper. And yet, it was like a floodgate had opened. What was it inside her that couldn't shut up and leave well enough alone? Her heartbeat knocked on her throat and yet she kept on going.

"Gender discrimination is a serious issue in our culture at large, and it would be nice if our school could be a leader, not a follower. A leader in trying to change things. To help people see it differently. If you're hell-bent on prescreening dresses, then it should at the very least be a rule that applies to everyone, to be both gender inclusive and less discriminatory. Aren't those things we all want for our community?"

Mrs. Ratliff rolled her eyes. "I don't need to look at a hundred photos of boys in tuxedos to know what a boy in a tuxedo looks like. It's not necessary. There are only so many hours in the day. Dresses vary, and people's idea of what's acceptable varies."

"'Acceptable' is subjective and value-laden. At least there should be an empirical scale, like skirt length in school on a normal day. It's measured in inches. Which at least lets you gauge for yourself. Basically, we can only wear dresses to prom that you personally approve of? That's totally unfair."

"That is the rule. You don't have to like it."

"No one said I have to like it, or put up with it, or keep quiet about it," Amber said. She had better leave before she dug herself in any deeper. She stood up and gathered her backpack. "Is there anything else?"

"I think that's been quite enough, Miss Harris-Rutledge," Mrs. Ratliff declared. "I've made my position very clear."

"Likewise," Amber muttered. She pounded the doorframe on her way out. *So many articles to write, so little time*, she thought.

Cole

"Hey," Cole said as Julio hopped into the car.

"Hey. Thanks for the ride, man."

"It's cool." Cole peeled out of the driveway. "Thanks for telling me we had to get on this tux situation early. I woulda been rolling up on prom eve like 'what can you rent me real quick.'"

"Same. You can thank Blossom. She's the one who told me we have to get measured for this ish."

"The things we do for love," Cole quipped. "Total bullship."

Julio glanced at him. "I'm doing it for love. I thought you were doing it for a night of fun. You into someone, for real?"

Cole grinned. "I meant love, like *love*." He pumped his fist suggestively.

"As I suspected." Julio smirked. "You're such a dog."

"You say 'dog,' I hear 'god,'" Cole answered. "This dyslexia's gotta be good for something."

Julio laughed. "You're such a mess."

"You don't even know." Cole cranked up the radio and gunned the engine. Music poured from the speakers, and they nodded along to the beat.

Julio was only giving him grief, Cole knew, like guys do, but did they really know each other well enough for that kind of slam? Maybe he was being oversensitive because today he sure as shiz felt like a mess. He had his probable dad's name and work address in a photo on his phone. Robert Clayton III, esquire.

Attorney at law, practice areas of specialty include real estate, wills and trusts, and insurance law. Alum of Butler University undergrad and Indiana University law. A quick internet search had given plenty of information.

The two rode in silence, Cole stewing in his own juice and Julio seemingly calm and lighthearted, bopping along to the music. They parked outside the tux rental shop, which was adjacent to a bridal boutique. As they headed in, a pretty young woman walked out with a large garment bag. Julio held the door for her.

Cole watched her backside as she headed for her car. She was . . . quite shapely. "Oooh, I'd definitely like to hit that," he murmured.

Julio glanced at him. "Yo, maybe there's a different way to say you think she's attractive?"

Cole laughed. "She's more than attractive. That's why I want to hit it. Think she'd give me her number?" He smoothed back his hair.

"Maybe take it down a notch?" Julio suggested.

Cole was confused. Most of his friends would've high-fived him and cheered him on. Obviously he wasn't likely to get anywhere with a hot older woman, but wasn't this the kind of thing guys said to each other to be cool? He looked back at the woman.

"Seriously? You're telling me you don't like the look of that ass?"

"You really are a dog, aren't you?" Julio shoved him through the door.

"Why does everybody keep saying that?" Cole said, legit kind of annoyed about it.

"You're right. It's an insult to dogs," Julio said with a laugh. "My point was, your way of talking about women skews a little misogynistic, don't you think?"

"I support women," Cole said. *But there's "women" and then there's the girls you bang.* If he was with any other friend, he might have said that part out loud, but Julio was making him feel like he shouldn't. "What's wrong with trying to get some?" he said instead. "It's kind of how we're wired."

"Yeah, there's nothing wrong with trying," Julio agreed. "As long as we do it with respect."

"No wonder you're still a virgin." Cole laughed.

"I, uh . . ." Julio shuffled his feet. His cheeks flushed.

Cole laughed again. "You know they all like a bit of bad boy, right?"

"What does that even mean?" Julio said.

"You know, like, they want you to be a little rough-and-tumble. They wanna roll their eyes at you and act all superior, and then jump your bones. That's how it always goes in the movies, right?"

Julio frowned. "Don't you think that's kinda messed up?"

"Why?" Everyone was saying that to him lately, too. It was getting his dander up.

"If we act like rutting cavemen, it brings us all down," Julio said.

Cole had an unwelcome flashback to Emmy saying *You scared me.* He shook it off. "Lay off me, okay?" he snapped.

"Okay." Julio held up his hands. "No harm, no foul. My friends and I try to call each other out when we hear one another being sexist. It happens. I thought you would want that too."

"Guess I have enough people giving me a hard time about things right now," Cole said. "I don't need to add to that list."

"Fair enough. You and I don't know each other that well. I just figured you'd get it . . . we're steeped in this culture of toxic masculinity that encourages us to act like horndogs. Or makes us feel like we're less than, if we're not all testosterone-forward."

"Tell me you've been spending time with my sisters without telling me," Cole said dryly.

Julio shrugged. "I mean, I guess that's why I even said it. You grew up around all these women. I thought you would understand where I'm coming from."

Cole felt a familiar stab of anger, a feeling that was suddenly all too close to the surface. "That's kind of the problem. All women, all over my life. I had to figure out how to be a guy entirely on my own."

Julio nodded as if he understood. But he couldn't, Cole knew. Not really.

"I'd want you to hold me accountable, too, by the way," Julio said. "There's a lot of toxicity out there. The more we catch each other, the more we learn."

"Fine," Cole said. *Whatever.*

Thankfully, Julio let it go after that. They went into the tux shop and got more measurements taken than Cole had ever known possible.

On the way back out, Julio said, "You wanna get a bite to eat or anything?"

Cole shook his head. "Nah, I'm gonna drop you off. And then I got another errand to run." He tried to sound casual, like it hadn't been in the back of his mind all day. Like the conversation with Julio hadn't been part of the impetus to push him over the last hurdle.

Today was the day. Finally.

He had the courage. He had the drive. He had the time.

He was going to meet his dad.

Blossom

Blossom sat cross-legged on the couch at the Harris-Rutledge house. Penney handed her a fresh scoop of warm Rice Krispies candy. They were eating it right out of the saucepan with the wooden spoon they'd used to stir it up. This was Penney's go-to solution for cheering up a moody kid. It nearly always worked, too.

"I told my mom that I'm definitely not going to do it," Blossom confided in the woman who was like a second mother to her.

"But?" Penney spoke the unspoken echo.

"But I want to. And we've been talking about it," she admitted.

"Talking is good. Keep talking. All you ever need to do is talk. Until you're over thirty."

"Argh," Blossom grunted. "I thought maybe you'd be cooler about this."

Penney grinned. "I'm the epitome of uncool. We know this."

"Stahp." Blossom rolled her eyes. Penney was by far the coolest of their three parents. Four parents, if you counted Colby, which Blossom generally didn't since he'd never lived with them all in the same way.

"Okay, so I'm the very most hippest, and I'm still telling you, keep it in your pants, sister. You'll never regret waiting."

Blossom frowned. "I thought y'all's mantra was 'no regrets.'"

Penney shot her a serious look. "None of us regret bringing you monsters to term. You know that."

"Yeah," Blossom muttered, around a mouthful of marshmallowy Krispies. They'd all heard this speech before.

"We chose you. Poopy diapers and sticky faces and the cost of orthodontia and all. Do you know what kind of discipline it takes to cut freaking blueberries in half so a baby doesn't choke? My god, now I'm having toddler flashbacks. What are you doing to me?" Penney melodramatically cupped her face.

"Now I see where I get my flair for theatrics," Blossom said.

Penney laughed. "Please, I'd never seen drama until I met your mother. You come by that honestly."

Blossom was skeptical. "My mom is the least dramatic person I know."

Penney cracked up. "Well, you didn't know her when she was seventeen and pregnant and getting kicked out of the house."

Blossom leaned into Penney's shoulder. "She wouldn't do that to me, would she?"

Penney smoothed Blossom's hair back. "Not in a million years."

"Promise?"

"I promise. Hon, I was being jokey before, but the reality is, it's possible for two things to be true at once. Regretting and not regretting. We can't go back in time and say we want things to be different, especially now that we know how wonderful you all grew up to be. But back then, when you were a clump of cells, merely the idea and promise of a person, it felt a lot more complicated. Your mom and I both wished like hell that the condoms had worked, okay?"

"Yeah." Blossom licked a drop of candy off her hand.

"It's not an easy thing to articulate, but I think you're mature enough to understand the nuance there. It doesn't make you any less wanted, or any less loved."

"I feel loved." That was the kind of thing she couldn't admit so directly to her own mom, so it was pretty great to have second moms to be gushy with.

"It was the toughest thing any of us ever did, and our lives would've been easier in many ways if things had gone differently. We want you to have easier lives than we had. Which is why I'mma go get a banana right now and you're gonna show me that you know—"

"Boo. Cool card revoked!" Blossom sat up, laughing.

"Hey, in my day, showing someone how to use a condom was the epitome of cool."

"Times change, old lady. Anyway, my mom's already put me through my paces. It's good."

"You're on birth control, too, right?"

"Mom took me to get a prescription a few months ago," Blossom hedged, leaving out one little detail: She hadn't started taking the pills yet. The little box sat on her bedside table, mocking her every morning. She knew she had to start taking them at least a week before having sex. Soon. Soon.

Blossom sighed. She hadn't been able to admit it to Julio, but he was right. The reasons holding her back were mostly in her head. The feeling of being ready-but-not-ready confused her. Her body wanted things. Her heart wanted things. But her brain kept screaming "Danger!"

"We probably won't even do it anyway," she added.

"Let me know if you do? Or when you're getting close?"

"Ew. That's so weird."

Penney shrugged. "You need people to talk about this stuff with. It's a lot to go through on your own. Boys are confusing."

"Even Colby?"

Penney snorted. "Twenty years in and I'm still like WTF is he thinking? Like, on a daily basis. Their brains are wired differently."

Blossom grinned. "You're lucky, you don't have to worry about any of this with Amber."

"I wish." Penney leaned over and kissed Blossom's forehead. "It's a mom's job to worry, no matter what. My offspring know how to wield latex with the best of them, by the way. All y'all's fluidity is enough to keep all of us on our toes."

Amber's voice called out from the kitchen. "Who's talking about fluidity? Guess I got here right on time." She scooted into the room carrying a massive plate of veggies and dip. "Oh, hey, Bloss." Amber set down the tray and draped her arms around Blossom's shoulders. "Ooh, Krispies!" she exclaimed, grabbing out a fingerful.

"Speak of the devil," Penney said. "How did the article go over?"

"Amazing. Everyone is talking about it. And then I got called to the vice principal's office and it got even more epic when she threatened me with detention for exercising my freedom of speech."

"The frick?" Blossom exclaimed.

"Right?" Amber chomped on a carrot stick. "EP-IC. I totally have my next article." She spread her hand through the air as if painting the headline. "Administration Denies Students First Amendment Rights."

"Oh, lord," Penney groaned. "This ends with me hiring a real attorney, doesn't it?"

"I think my mom can have that covered," Blossom assured her. Mina worked as a paralegal now and had recently taken the LSAT so she could apply to law school when Blossom went off to college.

"Mom, don't you have something to DO?" Amber said pointedly. "Like, somewhere else?"

"Sheesh. Apparently the skill of subtlety skips a generation," Penney grumbled, moving toward the door. She pointed back at Blossom. "You keep me in the loop." Blossom nodded, appreciative that Penney didn't air her private issues in front of Amber.

"Ugh," Amber scoffed. "I know you like her better than me, but Blossom's not your spy, Mom."

"Blossom brings me treats and respects my opinion," Penney retorted. "What's not to like?" She stuck her tongue out at her daughter and received a throw pillow to the face as a result.

Blossom simply laughed, knowing the exchange was deeply good-natured and all in fun. She reached for a celery stalk and dipped it, to offset the big hit of sweet she'd been taking from the Rice Krispies. Then she settled back into the sofa, prepared to receive the flood of information Amber was clearly about to release. Her pseudo-sibling was wound tighter than a top, and the only recourse would be to let her spin herself out. Prom dress code. Patriarchy. Sticking it to the man . . .

Blossom transferred the pan with the remaining Krispies from the far side of her to Amber's lap. "Okay, I'm ready," she said. "Let it out."

Cole

The office lobby was swank. It had small-town-business-office energy around the edges and in the bones of the place, but someone had brought in a fancy designer to make it look twenty-first century appropriate. The waiting area was all sleek white-leather furniture with black legs. The coffee tables were glass. The art on the walls splashy and metallic.

Ahead of him a young woman in a shocking pink sheath dress with a massive bow at the neck stood behind a high-topped white counter, looking like the check-in agent at a fancy hotel. She smiled as he entered.

To the right, a security guard stood at an identical high-topped white counter that resembled a concierge desk. He looked like a cross between a bouncer, a secret service agent, and a hitman, with muscles straining his clothing, an earpiece, and an all-black suit.

Cole scooted awkwardly past him and approached the neon receptionist. The cut of the dress was cute, he decided as he got closer, but it was loud.

"May I help you?" she asked warmly.

"Yeah." Cole swallowed hard. "I'm here to see Robert Clayton."

The receptionist clicked a few keys, then her welcoming face turned cool and neutral. "Do you have an appointment?"

"No."

"I see." She rolled her lips in. "I'm afraid Mr. Clayton only sees clients by appointment."

"Maybe he'll make an exception?" Cole suggested. "It's kinda urgent. I'll be really fast, I promise. I just need to see him."

"Are you an existing client, Mister . . . ?" Her voice trailed off, leaving him to fill in his name.

"No, I just need to see him. That's a really nice dress, by the way. Very eye-catching." Cole offered a grin he knew to be charming.

"Aww. Thanks, hon." The receptionist clicked a few more keys. "I'll see if someone else is available to speak with you."

"No, it has to be Mr. Clayton," Cole hurried to say. "That's who I was told to ask for."

"Oh, you have a referral?" the receptionist asked. "From whom?"

"No, not really. Not anything formal. Someone I know did business with him a while back, that's all." He was making it up as he went along.

"Mr. Clayton is very busy, you understand. I'd be happy to make an appointment for you." She clicked a few more keys. "Looks like he's booking out about two weeks for new clients."

Two weeks? Cole couldn't wait that long. If he had to stand in the lobby until Robert Clayton III came out at the end of the day, that's what he'd do. "I'm not exactly a new client," he said. "But it's very important. A personal matter."

"Well—" The receptionist frowned.

"I only need a few minutes. Not very long at all. Could you just check for me, please?" He put on the sad-hopeful face he used when asking for a favor from his mother. Tried-and-true at melting the hearts of women of a certain age.

"All right. I'll see if he has time." She punched a button on her large phone console. She spoke into her headset. "Hey, Jan.

Does Mr. Clayton have a minute for a walk-in? Yes. A young man. His name?" The receptionist glanced up at him.

"Cole."

"A Mr. Cole."

Cole opened his mouth to correct her but didn't. Progress was happening. The receptionist drummed her nails on a notebook as she waited. Presumably the other assistant was checking with the attorney.

"Have a seat, Mr. Cole. Mr. Clayton's assistant will be out to meet you when he's off his current call."

Cole breathed a sigh of relief. He perched on the edge of one of the pristine white couches, feeling for all the world like a toddler with sticky hands in someone's nice living room. A toddler wouldn't care, he reminded himself. But it didn't take away the queasy, awkward feeling.

A few minutes later a smartly dressed older woman emerged. "Mr. Cole?"

He stood up. "Yes." He nodded to the receptionist and followed the assistant back to a large corner office with the door standing open.

"Mr. Clayton will see you now," the assistant said.

"Thanks," Cole told her. "I really appreciate it." As she closed the office door behind him, he turned to face the man himself.

"How can I help you?" said Robert Clayton III, attorney at law.

Cole took a deep breath. What else was there to do but rip off the Band-Aid? "My name is Cole Brewster. I—I think I'm your son."

Robert Clayton III cleared his throat. "Excuse me?"

"I—" Cole's voice faded and he floundered. He'd said it once. Why was it hard to say again?

"Never mind. I heard you." Robert Clayton III stood up behind his desk. They were a similar height. Similar build. The way his hand looked as he pressed his fingers into the desktop was uncanny. Cole got chills.

"You're not supposed to be here," the attorney said. "Tell your mother she broke our agreement, and I'll see her in court."

"What agreement?" Cole blurted out. *See her in court?*

"She told you who I am. She wasn't supposed to."

So it was true. His mother had lied. His father had known. He tried to push down the surge of panic. And the surge of rage that followed it. *Stay focused on the problem at hand.* Cole took several gasping breaths.

In front of him, Robert Clayton III was dialing the office phone. "Security," he said simply, into the handset. Then he hung up.

"She didn't tell me. I found you on my own," Cole explained.

"That wasn't supposed to be possible. I'm afraid I'll have to ask you to leave."

The panic rose within him. He'd only just gotten close.

"I sent away for my DNA profile," Cole hurried to say. "That's how I found you." It was true but not the whole truth. "My mom has no idea that I'm here."

Robert Clayton III regarded him coldly. "Really. Then you should leave right now, and we should both forget this ever happened," he said. "Can you do that, Cole?"

It was the first time in his life he'd heard his biological father speak his name. The moment should have been momentous, and it was. Though it was also nothing like he'd imagined. He didn't know what to say.

Behind Cole the door opened. "Mr. Clayton?" the security guard inquired.

Robert Clayton III simply nodded.

"Mr. Cole, please come with me," the security guard said. "I'll show you out."

Cole allowed himself to be led from the office, down the hall, past the indifferent assistant, past the concerned receptionist, out onto the steps.

When Cole simply stood there, blinking at him, the security guard said, "You can make your way from here?"

Cole managed to nod, and the beefy man hesitated only for a second before retreating inside. Alone on the steps, Cole nodded again, to no one. *You can make your way from here?* The truth was, he had no freaking idea.

THEN

June 2005

Sheryl

Sheryl sat on a bench in the hallway, waiting. She took deep, calming breaths until the bustle of the lawyers' office stilled around her. Two men approached from the far end of the office suite, glancing at her as they crossed into a conference room. A few moments later, a dapper male assistant emerged from the same office suite.

"Miss Brewster, they're ready for you."

Sheryl glanced toward the conference room door. The meeting wasn't supposed to start until four thirty. It was only twenty-five after, and Tana had stepped down the hall to the restroom. "Um, okay. We'll be right in."

"We?" said the athletic-looking man. "You brought someone with you?"

"Yes, my friend . . ." Sheryl felt like her voice barely carried beyond her mouth. "The restroom. She'll be right—"

"I'll show her in," the assistant said.

Sheryl wanted to wait for Tana, but the assistant stood there expectantly. So she picked up her bag and followed.

The room was cold, as if the AC had been on full blast until moments ago. There was no sound emanating from the unit now. Sheryl had only seen the two lawyers enter the conference room, so she was surprised to see four men waiting for her. The lawyers, plus an older man who she guessed was Rob's father, and Rob himself. She froze in the doorway upon the sight of him.

"Please have a seat, Miss Brewster. This needn't take long," said the older man. He had to be Rob's father. Robert Clayton, Jr. The big-time lawyer. He conducted himself like someone who was used to getting his way.

Sheryl regretted not waiting for Tana. She assured herself she'd be along any minute.

"Have a seat, Sheryl," one of the other lawyers said. "We'd like to explain what's going to happen next."

He said it like what was about to happen was a foregone conclusion. But Tana had made her swear not to speak in the meeting unless Tana directly asked her to. So she pulled out a chair—the farthest from Rob that existed—and sat down without a word.

"We're here to offer you a financial settlement," the elder Clayton said. "In exchange for you dropping your charges against my son."

Sheryl said nothing.

"Do you understand?" the other lawyer asked.

Sheryl understood, but she wasn't sure if nodding constituted speech. So she glanced toward the door.

The elder Clayton pushed an envelope across the table at her. The envelope was unsealed. The gum seal flap was tucked over a cashier's check, in the amount of ten thousand dollars. Sheryl stared at it, trying not to react. Ten THOUSAND dollars? Her eyes nearly bugged right out of her head.

Mr. Clayton chuckled. "I take it the amount is agreeable?"

Sheryl said nothing. Tana had made her promise.

One of the other attorneys cleared his throat. "We're going to need you to say something now," he said. "Do you agree to the terms of the settlement offer?" He pulled out a stack of papers, marked with numerous little yellow signature flags. "If so—"

"Excuse you, Frederick," Tana said loudly, storming into the room like an avenging angel. "Where do you get off making an offer to my client outside of my presence?"

Sheryl breathed a sigh of relief.

Tana thumped her rather large, elegant briefcase down on the table and regarded the room. "Feeling exceptionally reptilian today, are we, gentlemen?"

"Tana Crow?" Mr. Clayton narrowed his eyes. "What are you doing here?"

"I'm representing Ms. Brewster."

"You?"

Tana glanced down at the check on the table and emitted a sound that was somewhere between a laugh and a scoff. "You're not nearly as worried about this situation as you should be." She placed one finger on the official rectangle and slid it back across the table.

Sheryl blinked. Ten thousand dollars? Pushed away? That was more cash than Sheryl had ever seen in her life by at least twenty-fold.

"It's a nuisance allegation." Mr. Clayton crossed his arms. "Obviously Miss Brewster knows we can afford to settle, which is why she set her sights on my son as a mark for her machinations." He studied Sheryl, maintaining a polite smile. "Well played, young lady. I barely begrudge handing a bit of cash to such a clever girl." He pushed the check back toward her. "Let's end this here, shall we?"

Tana ignored the check and took her seat beside Sheryl. "Clearly you didn't expect Ms. Brewster to have adequate representation in this matter, because this offer is a joke. Ms. Brewster isn't interested in a settlement. She will be pressing charges." Tana stood back up.

Mr. Clayton sat forward. "Bullshit."

The other attorney cleared his throat. Rob's eyes widened in surprise.

Mr. Clayton continued, unfazed. "This was clearly a settlement offer meeting. Your client showed up. She wants money. End of story."

"Ms. Brewster wants justice," Tana corrected.

"Mr. Clayton isn't denying that he had sexual relations with Ms. Brewster," droned the other attorney. "But he categorically refutes her claim that it was nonconsensual."

"The DA's office has a rape kit that says otherwise."

"The rape kit was inconclusive."

"In your opinion, Frederick. But the county is willing to prosecute based on the evidence in hand." She glanced at Rob's father. "Which Mr. Clayton well knows, or he'd not be making this offer."

"This has gone on long enough," Mr. Clayton barked. He glanced at Rob, then back at Sheryl. "What more do you want? Ten thousand. For a one-night stand? That's highway robbery, but let's end it there."

Sheryl swallowed hard. Ten thousand dollars. It was practically a year's tuition.

Tana sighed. "My client agreed to this meeting as a courtesy, which is certainly more than she owes your client. Your *son*," she corrected, emphasizing the relationship note.

"This case will never see the inside of a courtroom," Mr. Clayton blustered.

Tana stood firm. "I've spoken to the district attorney. The investigation is ongoing, but they do intend to prosecute."

Mr. Clayton shook his head. "The case will be dropped. Most are, when it comes down to a he-said, she-said misunderstanding on a date."

"You're drastically underestimating the evidence in hand," Tana said. "His DNA, her bruises. A jury will take one look and understand clearly what happened."

Mr. Clayton pierced Sheryl with an uncomfortable gaze. "I agree. They will take one look at this little slut and see the dollar signs in her eyes."

"If we are going to continue this conversation, you will treat my client with respect," Tana insisted.

Mr. Clayton met Tana's gaze. "This is a good offer. It spares everyone the pain and expense of a trial, and the damage to my son's reputation and the damage to Ms. Brewster's, for that matter."

"The situation has changed, Mr. Clayton." Tana reached into her briefcase and extracted a single sheet of paper. Sheryl recognized the Planned Parenthood logo in the top right corner. Her gaze cut toward Rob. This was the moment. This was how he'd find out—actions have far-reaching consequences.

Mr. Clayton's smug grin evaporated. He slid the page toward Rob without a word. His face whitened as he stared at the medical statement.

"Surely she's not keeping it."

"That's her decision."

Rob stared at Sheryl. She could feel his gaze upon her, and while she tried to pull her attention up to meet it, it was all too much. She kept her focus on a knot in the wood grain of the table in front of her. She thought she might be sick. His eyes on her brought back his hands on her, pressing, kneading. The weight of his knees on her inner thighs. A part of him was still inside her and knowing it made her gag deep in her throat. She choked down the emotion that rose up. Looking at Rob himself was still too much, but she forced herself to look at her rapist's father.

"I'm keeping the baby," Sheryl whispered.

Mr. Clayton had called her baby "it," and the protective surge of electricity that coursed through her when she heard it cemented what she already knew.

Tana smiled. "So, you see, Mr. Clayton, Ms. Brewster doesn't need a settlement. One DNA test and the young Mr. Clayton will be paying child support for the next eighteen years, in or out of prison. We'll see you in court."

"Tana."

Tana put her hand on Sheryl's shoulder. "Stand up. We're leaving."

"Tana, wait."

Sheryl stood up. She dared a glance at Rob, who sat with his head bowed.

"Come on," Tana spoke gently, but her hand on Sheryl's upper arm was firm. She steered her out of the room and down the hall, to the echo of Mr. Clayton shouting after them, "Tana, be reasonable!"

Penney

Penney was not looking forward to talking to Colby. That was pretty much a first. Normally she loved talking to him. They could spend hours together shooting the breeze. And it's not like it was always nonsensical or anything. She had some friends—acquaintances, really—who you could spend a whole evening with and have a great time but never actually touch on any topics of substance. Not politics, not emotions, not anybody's goals or anybody's dreams, just a whole lot of inane conversation and laughter. Colby wasn't like that. Colby was real. He could look her in the eye and ask something simple, and before she knew it, she was pouring her heart out and he was hanging on every word.

He was a serious guy, with hopes and dreams of his own, and here she was about to plop a big old cow on the tracks in front of him.

He clomped in through the kitchen door wearing his work boots. He would've been on his way home from work at this time on a Wednesday. They didn't usually see each other outside of school on weekdays because he worked at the farm and yard. It had been out of his way to come here today, but she'd said it was important and that's the kind of guy he was.

Colby swept off his cap as he crossed the threshold, revealing his close-cropped black hair. His edges looked very neat. He'd been to the barber in the last day or so. He looked windswept and handsome. As close to a romance novel hero as she could ever hope to land. Her heart ached for feeling lucky that he'd ever given her the time of day. Her stomach flipped nervously.

"Hi, Penney," he said. Sometimes he called her "babe" or "honey" or whatnot, but never when they were first meeting up. She loved that about him.

"Hi." She tipped her face up to meet his gentle kiss. She prayed it wasn't the last they'd ever share. She prayed he wouldn't flee. He wasn't like that. He wasn't.

Colby flipped the adjacent kitchen chair around and straddled it, folding his hands around two of the wooden posts that made up the chair back. He often sat like this. It was normal—the scritch of the swift flip, the shushing of his boots, the clatter of the chair legs back onto the tile. But this time Penney felt it slam like prison bars. She shook her head to release the image. It wouldn't shake.

She'd had a dream once about Colby being wrongfully imprisoned. Metal bars slamming between them, no choice but to walk away. She'd woken up sweating and sobbing at the thought of being ripped from him. At the injustice that could one day befall him because of his dark skin.

Now she wondered if it had been a premonition. Except it was her behind the bars. He was the one with the power to walk away.

Now Colby's hand was on hers. "Penney?"

"Yeah? Hi." She clutched at his fingers.

"You okay?" He smiled, eyes full of affection and concern. "You've never been this quiet."

"I'm sorry," she said. "I never wanted to put you in this position."

He frowned, confused. "What are we talking about? I don't understand." His gaze was impossibly warm. Penney felt herself melting. But she had to stay strong.

"I'm pregnant," she said.

Colby ran his hand over his scalp. "Sorry, what?"

"I'm pregnant."

Colby stared at her. Then he shook his head. "I'm just hearing . . . my head is full of static . . . this buzzing sound . . ." He started breathing harder.

Penney took his hands. "Shhh. I know. It's a surprise."

"You're pregnant? Like, with a baby?" His gaze dropped to her belly.

"Yeah, like that."

They sat together for a while, a long silence stretching out in time with the sunset.

"What happens now?" Colby finally said.

"I'm going to keep it. So, I'm going to be a mom and you're going to be a dad. That's what happens next."

"No, yeah." He blinked. "No, I know that. I figured that, based on your mom and all."

"She didn't get rid of me, so how can I?" She laid a hand on her stomach and shrugged. "I mean, I'm sorry. I know it puts you in a terrible spot."

Colby was still staring at her belly. "There's really a baby in there?"

"Still basically a clump of cells," Penney said. "But, yeah. There will be a baby in here pretty soon."

"We made a baby?" His disbelief would have been comical if the situation wasn't so life-alteringly serious.

"We're talented like that."

Colby jumped up suddenly. "I have to go." He practically shouted it.

Penney was taken aback. "Okay."

"I mean, I have to be . . . somewhere else for a minute."

"I understand."

"I have to go."

"Okay," Penney said.

"I have to be somewhere else."

"Okay," she whispered.

"Okay," he said. He hovered above her for a second, like maybe he was going to lean down and kiss her. He always, always kissed her goodbye. *Bye, baby.*

But now it meant something different. That minuscule clump of cells was changing everything.

Colby spun on his heel and rushed out. In the vacuum of his absence, Penney dissolved.

She grasped at the soft cotton place mat and hugged it to her face as the tears rained down.

What had she expected? Hearts and flowers and declarations of forever fatherhood? A promise to never leave her side? They were in high school. He had a scholarship. He had plans.

She laid her cheek on the table and stared woefully at the bars of the chair Colby had occupied.

Mina

"**What do you mean, pregnant?**" **Chip said.** "How can you be pregnant?"

"It's a sperm and an egg thing," Mina said dryly. "Remember health class?" Her knee-jerk response to him right now was flippant, which didn't make sense because inside she felt anything but lighthearted about the situation.

"But we used protection." He looked like she had smacked him in the face with a plank.

"Nothing's a hundred percent effective," Mina said. "Remember health class?"

"No," he said. "A condom is supposed to work."

"Yeah, but they don't always."

He continued to look poleaxed. "And you're sure? You took more than one test?"

"I've been to the doctor. I'm sure."

Chip shook his head. "That's messed up."

"Yeah."

They sat in silence for a while. Finally Mina broached the hard subject. "So, I made an appointment at a clinic—"

"No!" Chip exclaimed. "I don't believe in that. It's wrong."

Mina nodded. She'd made the decision not to tell him before going to the clinic. She knew he would have objected to her choice to terminate. But now, now that the baby was going to be real, she didn't have a choice.

"Some people change their beliefs in the moment, when they're really faced with the situation," Mina said. "Like all those pro-life senators who pay for their mistresses' abortions."

"People don't really do that," Chip said. "That's such liberal hype."

"It was just an example," Mina said. She didn't want to get into a discussion of politics with him. "The point is, it's one thing to think about abortion in the abstract, and it's another thing when you're facing it down."

"You can't get an abortion," Chip insisted.

"My parents are going to cut me off if I don't," she said. She was burying the lede, to be sure, but she couldn't help it, somehow.

"They can't do that," he argued. "What the hell?"

"I don't know if they really will," Mina said. "Or if it was just a threat to get me to do what they wanted." *Which is what I always thought I'd do in this situation anyway.*

"That's a messed-up ultimatum," Chip said. *Finally, something we can agree on.*

"I know."

"Shit," he said. "This wasn't supposed to happen." *Yup. Yup.*

"We decided to have sex. This is one of the things that can happen."

"So you're not, like, gonna keep the baby, right?"

"Yes, I am."

"I mean, I know you'll *have* it. You're Christian, like me. But you'll give it up for adoption."

Mina took a deep breath. "No, I don't think so."

Chip frowned. "But what about college? You're all excited about Kenyon."

So why does not having to go feel like such a relief? Mina could barely articulate the feeling to herself, let alone explain it. She rubbed her forehead. "It's insane to have a baby at eighteen. I know. I know. My parents are right."

"Whoa," Chip said. "Every life is precious. But also, like, you can't have a kid. Like, all by yourself. You're in high school."

"It takes two to make a baby, Chip," Mina said.

When he simply stared at her in response, she knew. If she went through with this, she was on her own. And what could she really expect? They'd had a few fun nights together over the course of senior year, but that was pretty much it. They weren't entirely a couple. They didn't plan their weekends together or exchange holiday gifts. They didn't walk down the hallway holding hands and staring moonily at each other. They were merely dating, hooking up, or whatever you wanted to call it.

"Adoption is not this magical fix. Do you know how many kids are waiting for a forever home? They wait in facilities and foster care, hoping someone will want them someday. I don't want to add to that problem."

"There's a lot of good homes out there."

"I can't stand the thought of wondering forever what happened to this little person," Mina said.

"But—"

"I know it doesn't make total sense," Mina admitted. "But it's what feels right to me."

"So, you're keeping it?" He looked confused.

"Yeah."

"So, what am I supposed to do?"

"Well . . . you're going to be a father. That's what I came here to tell you."

"No way," he said. "I'm going to college."

"Yeah, I know."

"I'm not going to change diapers and shit. How am I supposed to do that? What the hell?"

"I guess that's all I need to know," Mina said, standing up. "I had to tell you my decision. Now you get to make yours."

Penney

An hour later, Colby came back. Penney heard the knock on the door. She got up from the couch and muted the rerun episode of *ER* she'd managed to put on in the background.

"I'm sorry," he said. "I shouldn't have left like that."

"That's okay," Penney said. She didn't know what okay meant anymore. It hadn't felt great when he left, but she couldn't very well be mad at Colby for freaking out about a thing that was unquestionably, unimaginably freaky.

"I'm not expecting anything from you," she said. "I didn't get a chance to say that before."

Colby paced the living room. "I'm not going to abandon my kid."

"Oh."

"If I'm gonna be a dad, I'm gonna be one. Not like mine. I'm not skipping out."

"Okay." Penney felt a twinge of relief, though she tried not to let it turn into full-blown hope. She'd seen men promise her mother a lot of things, and then fail to follow through on nearly all of them.

"But I have to go to college," he said. "When I have my degree, I'll be able to provide for you proper."

"Okay."

"You have to finish high school," he said. "So you should stay here until the baby is born. One year. Is your mom okay with that?"

"Um, yeah. I think so?"

Colby nodded. "You might be able to earn enough credits in the fall to graduate early, or we can look into the GED." He paced across the carpet. "And then next year, you can join me at Purdue. I'll be living in the dorm freshman year, so it has to wait until fall. But then we can get an apartment. My scholarship has a housing stipend. It doesn't cover off-campus housing but it does cover married student housing, so there would be options. And . . ." He kept talking but Penney's brain had tripped like an overtaxed fuse.

Married. Penney felt light, like she was floating. Maybe the breath she was holding had finally been let out.

She moved closer to Colby, interrupting his breathless rant. "It's not up to you to solve the whole future today," she said. "You don't have to know all the answers."

"But I need you to know I will take care of you."

"I'm not asking you to take care of me."

Colby gazed at her with limpid distress. "But I love you."

"I love you too."

"We need a plan," he insisted.

"I agree."

Colby nodded. He reached into his pocket and pulled out a small notebook. "So here's the five-point plan: point one, we both graduate. Point two—"

"Are you kidding?" Penney grabbed the notebook from his hand.

"It's just a draft," Colby hurried to add. "I'm not trying to dictate. We can finalize it together but—"

Penney glanced at his handwritten notes. "*This* is what you've been doing for the last hour?"

"Well, I drove around a bit first," Colby said. "I think I ran a stop sign. People were honking."

Penney laughed. "You better not do that when we're in the car with you." Her hand found its way to her stomach. *We.*

Colby's hand covered hers. "I promise. Now, as I was saying—" He reached for the notebook, but Penney held it tight. She leaned up and kissed him. "What are you doing?" he mumbled.

"Appreciating you." She rested her forehead on his chest.

"Wait, but I'm not done," he protested. His arms were longer. He retrieved the notebook easily.

"Okay, Mr. Summa Cum Laude." Penney wrapped her arms around him.

Colby grinned. "You heard?"

"Third in your class? That's damn impressive, sir." Penney snatched the notebook from him again. "Once an honors student, always an honors student, I guess."

"What are you doing?" he asked, as she tucked the notebook in her back pocket.

"Someday you're going to do something famous or invent something cool," Penney said. "And there's going to be a museum exhibit somewhere about you, and this is going in it." She grinned, patting the notebook.

Sheryl

Penney and her boyfriend picked Sheryl up to bring her to graduation prep. Her foster mom was working, but she'd be at the ceremony itself. So would Tana. But the grads had to be there two hours in advance. It wasn't clear why. It really didn't take that long to park, get into the coliseum, and find your place in an alphabetical line.

The rehearsal yesterday had definitely felt like herding cats, but that was the point of rehearsal, so that you didn't have to practice again immediately beforehand. People were sheep, it turned out. Four hundred energetic sheep who were incredibly ready to never listen to another authority figure shout instructions about how to stand in a line.

"Thanks for the ride," Sheryl said as they pulled into the coliseum parking lot.

"No problem," Penney said, even though Colby was the one driving. And the one graduating. Penney sat between them on the Silverado's bench seat, fingering the billows of their gowns where they brushed against her.

Colby cut the engine and looked over at Sheryl. "You ready for this?"

"Ready to start the rest of our lives?" Her hand went to her stomach. "Sure. Yeah. Nope. Not remotely." She grinned.

Colby laughed. "Yeah, that about sums it up." He opened the door and got out.

They proceeded through the large parking lot. The coliseum was the massive arena where the local minor league hockey team played and where concerts would be held when the city was lucky enough to be a tour stop for someone relatively large-scale.

Colby and Penney held hands as they walked toward the looming venue. Sheryl tried to ignore the twinge in her gut at the sight of the two of them. Together. Supporting each other.

She averted her eyes as they kissed and parted, Penney heading toward the audience entrance and Colby heading toward the grads' area with Sheryl. She reminded herself she was lucky to have a cool couple like them as friends. That she wasn't as alone as she felt.

The feeling went away quickly as she and Colby moved through the air lock into the spacious arena. The hockey ice was hidden under the removable basketball floor at the moment, so they crossed easily toward the staging area. The air in here was definitely weird. As the ceiling lifted away above them, it felt like it took her breath away with it.

Sheryl followed Colby toward the honors section. He would be marching with the top ten, who would process in numerical order by rank. After that they'd do the high honors people, all alphabetical, then the honors people, all alphabetical. Sheryl was in the third group.

She knew from rehearsal the names of the two people standing next to her. Rob would be several spaces behind her, with five entire humans in between. Brewster. Brubaker. Byers. Cabot. Callaghan. Chambers. Clayton. She had counted the names in the program because he hadn't shown up for rehearsal. Yet another reminder that he was one of the special people, the obnoxious entitled ones who thought the normal rules didn't apply to them. Who couldn't deign to be inconvenienced by such a minor rehearsal.

"Here we go," Colby said. "Catch you on the flip side?" He popped his mortarboard onto his head, making sure the tassel hung on the correct side.

"Yeah," Sheryl said. "Let's do this thing." She smiled, trying to pretend that it didn't matter that he was leaving her alone to enter the fray. It wasn't his fault. She could handle it.

"Hey," Colby said, chucking her on the arm. "You got this."

He must've read something in her face, because Colby didn't know about Rob. She hadn't even told Penney the identity of the guy, especially because she was pretty sure Penney had guessed some of the shades of what had happened to her. With the offer of a settlement looming, Tana had warned her to be careful of who she told the whole story to. It could hurt her in court, too, if she stayed the course and pushed for a trial.

"I'm fine," Sheryl said. "Thanks." It had felt true when she started the sentence. By the time she finished it, the words were a lie.

There he was. Rob Clayton. Looking cocky and handsome and carefree as ever. Wearing the white gown, unbuttoned, with his mortarboard cocked at a jaunty angle. Showing off that he lived on the fringes of acceptability, and proudly so. Sheryl shuddered, taking her place in the alphabetical line. In a moment, Rob would be behind her. Able to study her at his will. She tucked herself between Sally Bonnie and Marvin Brubaker.

Exactly five people separated her and her rapist. She tried not to look too closely, but when push came to shove, she had to know where Rob was and what he was doing. Her gaze tracked his casual wanderings. He seemed to be waiting for the last possible moment to line up properly. As if to confirm he could buck the system and get away with it, as long as it happened just so.

Finally, he scooted his way into place. As he did, his attention swung forward exactly five spaces.

Sheryl met Rob's eyes. His gaze bored into her for one long, searing moment. And then he looked away. As though he'd barely seen her. As though it didn't matter. As though he wasn't one of the ten or so people on all of planet Earth who knew her biggest, most terrifying secret. As if he *wasn't* that secret.

He held her gaze for a matter of seconds, really, before he moved on. She was barely a blip on his radar. He couldn't hurt her now, Sheryl reminded herself. She turned her back on him.

Mina

It was all she could do not to cry. This was the moment she'd been waiting for all her life. The white gown, the mortarboard. Her maroon salutatorian stole and gold National Honor Society cords. The matching maroon dress and cream pumps she'd selected weeks ago to wear under the gown, so she'd look perfect in pictures. She'd had her hair done and spent a good hour in front of the mirror trying to smooth out the red blotches on her face. A minor breakout—pebbly and annoying and no doubt the result of the same raging hormones that made her boobs and her lower back ache—had cropped up on her cheeks and forehead earlier in the week. She'd skipped the mascara entirely because she'd felt on the verge all day. She lived on the verge now, it seemed. This moment had been meant to be perfect, and now it was anything but.

She felt a hand on her shoulder. Colby Harris stood behind her in line, third in the class. "You okay?" he said.

Truth be told, she felt nauseated. "It's probably nerves. Or hormones or something," Mina said, forcing a small laugh. She clutched at the stack of cards in her hand. Her salutatorian speech. It had been hard to write, under the circumstances. A happy welcoming message to send off her fellow grads into their bright exciting futures, while Mina herself . . .

Ugh. Her stomach flipped and flopped. She sucked on her tongue and tried not to swallow because it all felt very touch and go.

She was definitely pregnant. Her body felt flushed and weird. There was only a short time remaining until it would be absolutely too late to change her mind about the baby, and her parents weren't letting her forget it. They'd be sitting in the audience today, alternately radiating disapproval of her life choices and emanating proud waves at her for achieving salutatorian. The whole situation wasn't helping her nausea.

Mina tried to pretend Dad wasn't disappointed she hadn't made valedictorian in the end. Her attention to her studies had dropped off in the past two months, and it caused her to slip just enough to not pull off the top ranking. She didn't honestly care much. It was still a great achievement. How many people could say they were in the top two of the class? Exactly two. Not too shabby. Anyway, she had bigger problems now.

Sheryl

The graduation ceremony was everything Sheryl had expected. No more, no less.

When it was over, she joined the honors students at the reception at the coliseum roof garden. It would have been difficult to host a celebration for all four hundred grads and their guests in one place, but the school shelled out for a bit of sparkling cider to fete the top-tier students. Sheryl counted herself lucky to be part of that group, because there was no party awaiting her at home. No cake and ice cream and friends who would toss their hats into the air together and cheer.

Sheryl was standing awkwardly near the appetizers table, thinking about how the space they were in was somehow neither a roof nor a garden, when Penney and Colby rolled up on her.

"Hey," Penney said. "Looks like you did it. Congrats."

"Still standing," Sheryl agreed, raising her cider glass. She turned to Colby. "Nice job with the poem."

"Thanks," he said. As third in the class, he'd had the role of reading the poem the senior class had voted on to be their graduation theme piece.

"You have family coming?" Penney asked.

"My foster mom and another friend came," Sheryl said. "But just for the main ceremony." She'd meet Tana later for a celebratory dinner.

"Oh, look—" Penney nudged Sheryl and pointed.

Sheryl scanned the crowd for what she was talking about. A girl she thought she recognized was standing near the dessert table, mainlining chocolate-covered strawberries.

"Is she the one we saw at . . ."

"Ayup," Penney said.

"You know her?"

"Her name is Mina. The third musketeer."

"Ah," Sheryl said.

As they watched, Mina jabbed several more pieces of fruit into her face.

"Someone needs to go get that girl," Penney muttered. "And I think that someone is me." She drained her sparkling cider and handed the cup off to Colby.

As Penney darted away, Sheryl turned to Colby. "You have your hands full with that one, I take it."

"Happily," Colby said. "But don't kid yourself. Once Penney decides you're a part of her life, your hands will be pretty full too."

Sheryl smiled. She could handle that.

NOW
March 2024

Blossom

"Hurry up, Bloss! We're going to be late," Mina called up the stairs.

"Working on it!" Blossom called back. She scooped up a glob of leave-in conditioner and rubbed it all over her hands. She raked her fingers swiftly through her hair.

She should have started getting ready sooner, but she'd lost track of time. She'd spent the morning poring over the new students' page on Harvard's website yet again. There was so much information to absorb about housing options and class schedules and academic requirements. Her departure was still five months away, but between now and then there were all kinds of deadlines and decisions to make. She dedicated her weekend mornings to filling her desktop file with downloaded info documents and campus maps and carefully labeled screenshots of information she wanted to track.

"Clothes and go, hon," Mina urged from below. "Let's get a move on."

"We're only going next door," Blossom said. "How late can we be?" She emerged from the upstairs bathroom, still braiding her damp, curly hair. She glanced over the railing at her mother, who stood in the entryway holding a casserole.

"It's eleven right now," Mina said. "Time to go."

"Is that the broccoli and cheese thing?" Blossom asked, sniffing the savory air. The casserole must have just come out of the oven. "Smells great."

"Put on your pants and let's go."

"Everyone at this party has seen me without pants," Blossom muttered, sliding out of earshot. But Julio would be attending their weekly family brunch, so she didn't want her mother to hear her say that. "If you're so antsy, you could go ahead and I'll meet you over there in five minutes," Blossom called as she buttoned her blouse.

"If I don't wait it'll be more like fifty," Mina retorted. "Get a move on, kiddo."

"Fine," Blossom called. She was minutes from ready, but she liked to take her time, thank you very much. She grumbled at her mother in her head as she pulled on a floral skirt and cream tights. She had these new-ish beige boots that she was totally digging lately, and they would go perfectly.

Moments later, Blossom scampered down the stairs. She offered a twirl for outfit approval. "Very nice," Mina said, levering open the front door.

"Hmm. Your judgment can't be trusted right now," Blossom said. "You just want us to go. I may need to study myself in the mirror a few minutes longer . . ." She made like she was going back upstairs.

Mina rolled her eyes and used the casserole dish to catch Blossom in the midsection and steer her out the door. "Beautifying time is over," she declared. "If Julio isn't dazzled, he doesn't know a good thing when he sees it."

"Oh, he definitely does," Blossom answered. "Don't you worry." She crossed the porch and opened the adjacent front door. "Hello, hello!" she called. "We're home!"

Sheryl's place did feel like home to Blossom, as much as their own did. She and Mina had lived in this half of the duplex with Sheryl and Cole until Blossom was almost ten. The decor hadn't changed much in the intervening eight years.

A welcoming cheer went up from the crowd gathered in the living room and kitchen. Blossom felt the familiar jolt of warmth and surprise. It wasn't a huge place, and the family had grown considerably over the years—both in size and in numbers.

Cole, sitting on the couch beside Amber's dad, was so tall now that his legs stretched all the way under the coffee table and came out the other side. Curled up between them, making himself right at home between his idols, was Amber's nine-year-old brother, Sterling. The three seemed to be arguing about a football video game they all loved but were banned from retreating to the basement to play until the meal had concluded.

Mina had joined Penney and Amber in the kitchen, sharing hugs and kisses all around. Amber's oldest younger sibling, the budding pastry chef, was perched on one of the kitchen bar stools, squeezing icing out of a piping bag onto something that looked like Penney's famous coffee cake.

"Home sweet home," Amber said, popping out of the bathroom and draping her arms around Blossom.

"Julio's not here yet?" Blossom asked.

"Carmen's picking him up, remember?"

"Yeah, I just assumed she was the punctual type."

"It's like two after," Amber said. "You just assume everyone else should get places before you because you're always late."

"True facts," Blossom admitted. She leaned on her pseudo sibling and sighed.

"How you be; how you do?" Amber asked.

"Fair to middling," Blossom answered. Her mood seemed to dip and shift, depending on how hard she was thinking about the future at any given moment.

"I can't believe you still say that." Amber laughed. "What is that even from again?"

"I don't even remember." Blossom laughed too. "Some old-fashioned phrasing from a movie or something. I always thought it was funny."

"That, I remember," Amber said. She leaned her head on Blossom's shoulder. "Big day," she added. "Bringing the sig-ots to the family brunch."

"What were we thinking?" Blossom groaned, taking in the enthusiastic loving chaos unfolding in front of them.

When they were babies, their three moms had shared Sheryl's half of the duplex she owned. Back then, the half Mina and Blossom lived in now had been rented out to strangers. When the kids were nearly five, Penney and Colby had gotten married and moved into the other half. But they kept on having babies and so their family quickly outgrew the three bedrooms.

Now, Penney and Colby had their own house a couple of miles away, and Amber had three tiny siblings to wrangle. Speak of the devil . . .

"Blossie, Blossie!" The youngest of the Harris-Rutledge crew—six-year-old Diamond—twirled up to her, appearing out of nowhere. Perhaps she'd been hiding behind the front window curtains?

"Pretty," the child declared, petting the flowers on Blossom's skirt. Then she stuck her arms in the air. "Up?"

Blossom smiled and scooped the girl into her arms. "Ugh," she groaned. "Someone has been eating heavy rocks!"

"No, I haven't." Diamond giggled.

"You haven't?" Blossom acted surprised. "Then I guess you must be growing."

"Yes. Daddy says I'm going to be tall like a WNBA player!"

Amber laughed, waving a hand over her own short-to-average frame. "Keep dreaming, sis."

"Am too," Diamond insisted.

"Are not," Amber teased.

"Am too!"

"Okay, sure," Amber agreed. "Maybe Mom and Dad saved up all the tall genes they had and gave them to you."

Diamond looked smug. "Told ya!"

Blossom laughed as the doorbell rang behind her.

"Squee!" Amber said in a mock-delirious tone, causing Blossom to laugh even harder. Amber spun toward the door and let in Julio and Carmen. Coming up the steps after them was Tana, Sheryl's longtime friend and everyone's favorite adopted auntie.

"Hey, y'all," Amber said. She kissed Carmen, hugged Tana, and pounded fists with Julio.

"Gotta go down," Blossom told Diamond.

"No." The small girl clung to her.

"Yup. Gotta." Blossom slid her to the floor. "But you can be the first to come meet my boyfriend. This is Julio. Julio, this is Diamond."

Julio stuck out his hand. "Pleased to meet you, Diamond."

Diamond regarded him for a few moments. Then she raised her arms in the air toward him. "Up?" she said.

Amber, Blossom, Carmen, and Tana all laughed.

"Guess you got the Diamond stamp of approval," Amber said. "That's the highest praise we've got." She took Carmen's hand and led her into the gathering.

"Hey," Julio said, kissing Blossom on the cheek.

Blossom brought Julio in and introduced him around. They nibbled on Amber's prepared appetizer tray for a while, then shifted into the full meal around the dining table. Even with both leaves put in, the table was barely big enough for thirteen.

So Cole and Julio carried up the square folding table from the basement and pushed it against the end.

Tana had brought a fresh small tablecloth to replace the one damaged in last week's cranberry punch fiasco. "Seemed prudent not to go with white for the kids' end of the table this time." She laughed, whipping out a red one.

"Good thinking," Sheryl agreed. She helped Tana spread it over the table.

As they settled in to eat, the conversation turned to Amber's articles.

"The whole school is talking about it," Carmen boasted.

"It's been epic," Amber admitted, with flushed cheeks. "I've never been so popular."

"Who knows? If you keep pushing, they might have to change the school's prom policy."

"I'm definitely going to write a second article, but I think we need a bigger statement, too," Amber mused. "Something more people can get involved in."

"Like what?" Blossom asked.

"I don't know," Amber said. "A real protest. Something visual. Actionable. But also easy. Nobody has time to march in a picket line, or anything." She shrugged. "I'll think of something."

"That's our girl," Colby said. "Leading the charge."

"She's always been like this, you know," Penney said proudly. "Pushing the envelope since the day she was born. She was—"

"She was two weeks early, don'tcha know," Blossom and Cole chorused in unison.

Their moms all laughed.

"Oh, I've said that before, have I?" Penney quipped.

"Once or twice," Amber groaned, burying her face in her arm. After a moment of recovery, she picked up her head and raised one finger on the other hand. "But we'll show the administration we are not to be trifled with."

"You go, girl," declared Mina.

"Eww, that's so turn-of-the-century, Meen," Amber complained.

"Get it, ho," Mina corrected, giving a dramatic neck waggle. "Is that better?"

The whole table cracked up.

"Quit while you're ahead, babe," Penney said, patting her arm.

Everyone laughed harder.

As the conversation swirled around them, Blossom looked over at Julio. He was smiling, listening, watching it all unfold. She knew he was part of a large, loud, loving family himself. He looked comfortable. At ease. She hoped it was how he was feeling, too. It was nice to have him here.

She shifted her leg to the side, pressing her calf against his. Feeling the touch, he glanced at her.

"Hi," she mouthed.

"Hi," he answered. "This is great."

"Yeah," she said. "And you're great."

He winked at her and held out his hand. Under the table, just between them. Blossom laced her fingers between his and smiled.

Cole

Family brunch was always a really fun time, but today it had been all he could do to get through it. Colby had even asked him what was wrong when they went downstairs to play video games. He'd thought Cole seemed "moody" or upset about something. But he couldn't really talk about it. Not yet. Maybe not ever.

He didn't want to talk, but he did want information.

When brunch was over and everyone was gone, Cole took a deep breath and barged into Sheryl's studio. "Hey."

"If it isn't the fruit of my loins."

"Ew, Mom."

Cole skirted a stack of canvasses and moved closer. "Studio" might have been a strong word. It was the back corner of the basement, a "room" built out of boxes, separating her work-space from the area where the old couch and flat screen were set up for his video game consoles. Generally, it wasn't that much of an issue that they had to share the basement. His mom mostly used the studio during the workday when he was at school, and even if they wanted to both be in there, she just wore head-phones to tune out the sound of his blasting. He would've liked the area to be entirely his, to turn it into his bedroom even, so she could move her studio upstairs, but she needed access to the utility sink, so that suggestion had been a no-go.

Now Cole stood awkwardly in the neutral zone between her space and his, hesitating.

"Did you need something?" Sheryl asked. "I'll be done in a little bit."

"Tell me about my dad," Cole blurted out.

Sheryl ducked her chin for a moment, then swept her paint-brush over the canvas. "Sweets, I'm in the middle of something."

"I don't care."

"Whoa, check the 'tude, dude." Sheryl tossed him a mildly scolding look over her shoulder, then smiled.

Usually her dorky mom-isms cracked him out of stewing anger or frustration. Not today.

"It's weird how you never talk about him."

Sheryl frowned. "Is it? He hasn't been a part of our lives since well before you were born. How much could I have to say about him?"

"MOM."

Sheryl put down her paintbrush. "You haven't asked about him in years. Why now?"

"The answers you gave when I was little don't make sense anymore."

"There's not that much more to say," Sheryl explained. "I wish there was. I wish I could give you something with meaning about who he was, but I can't."

"You could," Cole muttered. "You just won't."

"Cole." Her tone was weirdly stern, out of nowhere, like he'd spoken the accusation directly. So he might as well speak it.

"You're lying."

"Cole—"

"The next thing you say had better not be a lie," he said. "You think I can't tell, but I can."

"Where is this coming from?" Sheryl asked. She seemed as upset and confused as he felt, but she had no right to. Not after keeping the truth from him all these years.

"You don't want me to know who I am!" Cole shouted. "Or maybe you don't want to share me. You want me all to yourself, and that's sick."

"That's not it at all."

"You know who he is. You've always known."

Sheryl took a deep breath. "Cole, if I could tell you who your father is, I would."

Liar.

"Whatever, Mom. I didn't need your help to find him anyway." He stormed out of the studio and bounded up the stairs two by two.

"Cole!" Sheryl scrambled after him. "Wait, what?" She caught up to him in the space outside the kitchen. "What do you mean?"

Cole whipped around. "I know who he is now. I've even seen him."

"You can't do that." Sheryl stretched her hand toward him.

"Like hell."

"Please wait." Sheryl burst into tears. "You can't."

"What better way to find out who he is than to meet him?"

Sheryl clasped her hands tight. "I'm so sorry, Cole, but I'm not the one laying down the law here. I need you to hear me. Legally, you can't go looking for your father."

"How can that be?" People did it all the time. Mail-order DNA tests were all the rage in the media and online. Adopted kids all over the place were finding out who their biological parents were. Why should he be different?

Sheryl twisted her hands. "You're right, okay? I owe you this explanation. I—I should've known I couldn't hide things from you forever. You're growing up so fast and I never wanted to hurt you."

Cole's mind spun a mile a minute. "I found a check stub in

your file cabinet," he admitted. "He's been paying you? Child support?"

"No," Sheryl corrected. "I mean, sort of . . ." She hung her head. "We need to sit down. We need to talk about this properly. I need you to understand why you can't go looking for him."

"Robert Clayton the third, attorney at law," Cole recited, his voice cold and steady. "I told you, I've already found him."

Sheryl moved toward him. "Keeping his identity a secret was not my choice."

There it was. The truth. She had lied. Kept him a secret. Kept half of who Cole was at bay all his life. He felt sick.

"I don't want to hear it," Cole said. "I've heard enough." He started toward the upstairs.

Sheryl called after him. "Fine, you can walk away from me right now. But I need you to swear to me, on everything we hold dear, that you won't reach out to this man or try to contact him in any way until you and I have had this talk. Swear to me, Cole. Swear it."

He pounded his way up the stairs without another word.

Amber

Blossom and Amber took a turn through the department store's junior section. Every dress in sight was super short, sequined, and strappy.

"We're not going clubbing," Amber complained. "Plus, none of this would be Ratliff-approved."

"It sucks that we have to care about that."

"Tell me about it," Amber grumbled. Her second article had gone over exactly as well as the first. Hugely popular with students, hugely not with Mrs. Ratliff. Amber was now on her permanent shit list.

"Let's try the misses section," Blossom said. "I'm hoping for, at minimum, a cap sleeve."

"We could learn to sew," Amber mused. "But I'd probably prick my finger on the needle and fall asleep for a hundred years."

"Last I checked, you don't need an enchanted needle to sleep for a hundred years."

Amber laughed. She affected her best Liam Neeson impression. "I have a very particular set of skills . . ."

Blossom laughed too. "Hey, speaking of making your own dress . . . I saw online that some girl made her dress and her date's tux out of duct tape to win a contest. She won a scholarship from the duct tape company after she posted the picture."

"A dress out of duct tape?" Amber sounded skeptical.

"Yeah, no fabric underneath or anything. She used up like eight entire rolls of pink duct tape for her dress and I-forget-how-many black and white rolls for his tux. It was pretty cool."

"Floor-length?" Amber asked.

"Short. And strapless. Definitely not Ratliff-approved."

"Ugh. You had my hopes up there for a minute."

By this point, they had arrived in the evening wear section. Some of the options here were better. Definitely more fabric on display, overall.

"So, how are things going with Julio?" Amber asked. "You two still hot and heavy?"

"Oh, you know." Blossom flipped through a rack of spaghetti straps.

"Well, I don't know," Amber countered. "That's why I asked. I mean, who am I to try to guess what goes on between heteros?"

"Why do you have to say it like that?"

"Heteros?" Amber asked. "I mean—is there something you haven't told me?"

"'Hot and heavy,'" Blossom corrected. "You make it sound so gross."

"Okay, I was going for sexy. But I'm sorry." She paused. "Seems like I hit a nerve there."

"No, it's fine." Blossom turned toward a rack of ball gown skirts. "These look fun." The skirts came in a variety of colors, all ranging from shimmery to sparkly.

"Then you have to get a top to go with it," Amber said. "That's two things to pick out."

There was a row of such tops. Mostly black or white, some strappy, some strapless, with varying patterns of sequins glitzing them up.

"These could be cute," Blossom said, pulling one and holding it to her chest. "Don't you think?"

"Yeah, actually, that could be perfect for you," Amber agreed. Not so much her own style, but, hell, she was on the fence about wearing a suit like Carmen. It felt like what she should do. It felt like what she should *want*. But truthfully, they were kind of opposite in that way. Carmen had the curvy femme body, but her style skewed more butch. She loved to play up her assets, but in a masculine-inspired way. Amber had the more androgynous appearance—slim hips, flat chest, shaved head, and yet when it came to a prom outfit, she wanted something she could twirl in. She halfway hated that about herself, but there it was. If she *had* to go to prom, she was gonna do it girly.

Blossom chose several of the glitzy tops and a handful of ball gown skirts to try on. The girls headed to the dressing room. Amber planted herself on the bench in the corner, leaning back as needed to avoid the whipping fabric. Blossom was not exactly a streamlined dresser, and flying tulle could cut a bitch.

"So . . . you didn't really say what the thing is. With Julio," Amber pointed out. "You guys okay? You seem like you're looking forward to prom and everything."

"Yeah, we're fine. It's not like that." Blossom smoothed the eggplant skirt over her hips. "This is gorgeous."

"It's perfect for your butt," Amber agreed. "The color is great. So Julio . . . ?"

Blossom sighed. "Which top do you think, with this one?"

Amber sighed too. She could take a hint, and Blossom had dropped several. No boy talk. "Try the strapless," she said.

They stared at Blossom's reflection.

"I love it," Blossom said.

"Princess level," Amber agreed. "Try one of the other tops, just for comparison."

Blossom tried several more combinations, but none rose to the level of the shimmery purple skirt paired with the strapless sequin top.

"So this is it," she said. "This is what he'll see me in."

"He won't be able to take his eyes off you," Amber assured her. "Not to mention his hands."

"Unzip me," Blossom demanded, holding her hair up. Amber did.

They packed up the extra items and cleared the dressing room.

"We still have to do you," Blossom reminded Amber.

Amber shook her head. "I need a different store."

They meandered in search of a cash register.

"Did you mean it, about Julio not being able to keep his hands off me?" Blossom asked.

"Sure," Amber said. "You're gonna knock him out."

"It's such a thing, right? To lose your virginity on prom night?" Blossom tried to sound casual.

Well, that took a turn, Amber thought. "Um . . . it can be a thing, I guess?"

"It's romantic, right?"

"Romance is in the eye of the beholder. Carmen thinks it's romantic when I show up with snacks. I think it's romantic when she reads out loud to me. We're nerds."

Blossom rolled her eyes. "You're *such* nerds."

"If dressing up for a dance is what does it for you, then I think that makes you one of the cool kids, B."

"That seems highly unlikely."

"I don't know. You two have some game." Amber tossed

Blossom a curious side-eye. "Are you thinking about prom night being, you know, IT?"

"Maybe."

"Oooh," Amber gushed. "That's big."

"I said, 'maybe.'"

"You don't have to put a weird timetable on it, B. Why does prom night have to be such a big deal? Why so much pressure there? Who flippin' cares?"

Blossom deflated. "You think it's totally cliché, huh?"

"Doesn't matter." Amber shrugged. "The point is, you should do it when you're ready, not when society tells you to. Buck the system, Bloss. Fuck him now, fuck him later, fuck him never. It's all good." Amber grabbed Blossom's arm. "I mean like, *really* good."

Blossom slapped the air with her hand, trying to quiet Amber. There were *people* around, for gosh sakes. How embarrassing. She grabbed Amber's arm and pulled her to the empty side of the checkout counter, away from the clerk.

"So, you've had sex with Carmen?" she whispered.

Amber sighed. "The idea of virginity is so heteronormative."

"So that's a yes?"

"That's an 'it's non-binary.' Like everything else about me." Amber did a little dance and dragged her hand across the Tensabarrier belt that formed the checkout line.

"I don't know what that means."

"I'm saying, we've done stuff. Kissing, touching. When I'm at the GYN and she asks if I'm sexually active, I say yes, with one partner."

"So you *have* had sex."

"Straight couples have this idea that sex is one thing. There's so much more to life than a penis in a vagina."

"Ugh. You make it sound so crude."

"That's what it is, though. You want his penis in your vagina. Ain't nothing wrong with that, baby." Amber placed her hand over her heart. "I mean, I don't personally understand it, but the heart wants what the heart wants . . . and the vag wants what—"

"Stahp," Blossom groaned. "Thank god we don't live together anymore. I'd have to move."

"Don't act like you don't love me." Amber threw her arms around Blossom. The sisters-but-not-sisters thing really had its advantages. Not living together anymore made them only barely get on each other's nerves. She kissed the side of Blossom's head.

"Your stock is going down as we speak."

"Nonsense. Want me to send Carmen to talk to Julio? She can give him some good pointers." Amber winked. "Penis-less pointers, if you know what I mean."

Blossom flushed bright red. "I will kill you."

"You'll thank me." Amber laughed. "OMG, I didn't know you could blush that hard. Look at those cheeks."

"I want other things too, you know," Blossom said.

"Exactly." Amber tugged her arm. "One of which is looking pretty for Julio, regardless of how the rest of the night goes. Which you can't do if we don't actually buy the dress." She led Blossom back to the checkout line.

"We could try that funky alternative store for you," Blossom suggested as the clerk handed her the garment bag and receipt. "The one next to the Mrs. Fields."

Amber nodded as they moved away from the checkout counter. "And since we'll be right next to the Mrs. Fields . . ."

"You know it." Blossom grinned. "We definitely deserve a small treat after surviving this retail hellscape."

"Well, what are we waiting for?"

Cole

He could smell the buffalo sauce from the wings wafting in from the hallway before his mother even knocked on the door. He'd been planning a hunger strike until after she went to bed, but this temptation was weapons-grade.

"It's your favorite." Sheryl spoke through the door when he didn't answer her knock.

"Leave it in the hall," he snapped.

"No dice. You don't have to talk to me, but I need to lay eyes on you."

"Fine," he said.

"I'm coming in."

"I said, fine." He was lying on his bed, staring at the ceiling.

Sheryl entered slowly. She surveyed the room, then placed the box of wings on the least-cluttered edge of his desk. "I know you're stubborn," she said. "So I didn't want you to starve."

He withheld his thanks out of spite. The wings smelled damn good. He'd scarf them in record time.

His mom smiled sadly at him and moved toward the door.

"Would you have ever told me?" Cole blurted out, just as she'd reached the hallway.

"No." Sheryl turned back to face him. When he glared at her, she shrugged. "You wanted the truth."

"If you were never going to tell me, why did you just tell me?" he snapped. He was mad about it. Mad that she had lied.

Mad that she had told the truth. Mad that he now knew something he didn't want to know. The contradiction was a paradox. But his reasons didn't cancel one another out. They were exponential. Mad on top of mad on top of mad.

"You've given me no choice," his mother said. "You needed to understand. I've made some mistakes in my life—"

"Like getting pregnant?" Cole's skin stung. He'd asked for the truth she'd been hiding. What if it was all a basket of regrets?

"Jesus, Cole. No." She moved toward the desk chair. "Can I sit down?"

"Spit it out, Mom."

"What you're asking is bigger than you realize," Sheryl said. "You have to let me explain."

How hard could it be to tell him about his dad? Geez. Cole scooted upright and faced her. He crossed his arms.

Sheryl twisted her hands. "Legally, you can't go looking for your father, because legally he's no longer your father. He signed away his parental rights as part of our arrangement."

Arrangement? Cole's heart sank like a stone. Some part of him had still been hoping his father never even knew he existed. Now it seemed the opposite. His father had wanted nothing to do with him, to the point of signing papers.

"What I have to tell you next is difficult, Cole."

How could it get worse?

"I made up the story about meeting him at a college party. Rob and I went to high school together. He was my prom date."

Then why lie? Cole's teeming rage thrummed in his throat.

"That night, he was drinking a fair bit with his friends," Sheryl said.

"So that much was true," Cole said.

"Yes, but not what happened next. I hadn't planned to have

sex with him. We didn't know each other that well, I didn't think. And not in that way. He'd been my science lab partner, and a friend, or so I thought."

Uh-oh. An alarm bell went off in the back of Cole's mind.

"It never occurred to me that he would expect . . . that he would try—" Sheryl shook her head and shrugged. "I guess I was a little naive maybe, but to me, it was basically a first date. I was nervous thinking that he might kiss me. I thought we might make out a little."

She stared into space for a moment.

"Anyway, he wanted something more from me. He thought he deserved it. I was the foster kid with the clothes that barely fit. I was probably blatantly desperate for attention and affection, and he gave that to me. And I fell for it, hard." She shuddered.

"So?" There was another shoe left to drop. He could feel it hovering.

"I'm avoiding saying it, Cole, because I never wanted you to know that this happened to me." Sheryl took a deep breath. "Rob Clayton raped me. On our prom night."

Cole could barely breathe.

"It was terrifying. The way it happened, so fast and unexpected. And then having to report it while I was still reeling from the shock. It was truly awful."

Cole sat, frozen.

"At first, I planned to press charges against him. I don't know what would have happened if we'd made it to court, but his family is very wealthy. They offered me a cash settlement. But I had to sign a nondisclosure agreement. It meant I could never tell anyone who your father is, or that he had raped me. Not for the rest of my life."

"And you took it?"

Sheryl nodded. "Once I found out I was pregnant, I needed a way to provide for you. If I could have done that and still pressed charges, I would have. But I wanted you to have a shot at a decent life. I had nothing."

"But it was so long ago," Cole said. "Why does it matter anymore what you tell me?"

"If I break our agreement, he could take everything we have," Sheryl said. "Sue me for breach of contract."

Cole swallowed hard. *Tell your mother I'll see her in court.* That hadn't been an empty threat. And he was an attorney.

"I'm so sorry, Mom," Cole said. He didn't know where to begin.

"I kept his identity a secret from you because I had to. Cole, even Mina and Penney don't know his name."

"They always backed up your story," Cole said.

"You've asked them?" She sounded surprised.

He felt a little sheepish all of a sudden. "I've always wanted to know who he is."

"I know, baby," Sheryl said. "It breaks my heart that I was never able to give you a father. And it breaks my heart all over again to have you know the truth."

"It's okay, Mom. You did the right thing." Cole kept his voice even, but now he was the one lying. The answers hadn't made him less angry; they'd transformed his whining infant rage into a storming, stomping giant. He wanted to defend his mom. He wanted to confront his dad. AKA his mom's rapist. Ew. Everything about it was too much to take.

Cole remembered the cold expression on Robert Clayton III's face as he looked at Cole. Barely glanced at him, really.

What was Cole, in his eyes? A monument to a huge mistake?

A reminder of the money he'd lost over the years in the settlement? A relic from another time?

There'd been no interest, no affection in his gaze. Cole hadn't wanted to admit how much that hurt. And now it hurt tenfold.

What was he to his mother? A reminder of the worst night of her life? A ticket to financial stability? He'd always known he was an accident. A mistake. But now he felt that tenfold, too.

"I'd like to be alone now," he told Sheryl.

"I love you, Cole. So much." She stood up and left, as he'd requested.

Her presence hadn't been helping, but her absence didn't help either.

Cole snatched up the box of wings. Scarfed them in record time. It took the edge off his hunger, but none of the weight off his mind. He was raging. His stomach was tight and his thoughts were racing. He needed to chill the fuck out. He needed a serious distraction.

No, he knew exactly what he needed. He reached for his phone. Time to call a girl, blow off steam.

Amber

"I got a dress," Amber told Carmen over the phone. "It only took us all dang afternoon and four different stores, but I got one."

"Ooh, I bet you look hot in it," Carmen said. "Can't wait."

"It's coming up so soon," Amber said. "You don't have long to wait."

"Did you take your Ratliff picture?" Carmen asked.

"Can't wait to show it to her first thing in the morning," Amber said. "Cap sleeves, square neckline, and hem pooling down to the floor. It's chaste as hell. She's going to love it."

Carmen laughed. "Seriously?"

"My mom's going to hem it," Amber said. "There's no way I'm wearing four-inch heels."

"I bet it's great," Carmen said.

"Yeah, now all I have to do is resist the urge to cut a trap door in the arse. Like one of those old-fashioned onesie pajamas with the butt flap."

"My family wore those one Christmas. My mom was super excited about it. We did that trendy, matching PJs for the holidays thing."

"Exactly once, I'm guessing." Amber laughed.

Carmen laughed too. "And barely that. My dad was totally NOT having it. They were red plaid, with a huge bear head on the chest and said *Beary Christmas* in script underneath. But

Mom didn't notice that there was writing on the back too." Carmen coughed back a chuckle as she relayed the memory. "The butt flaps said *Bear bottom*."

Amber howled. "Best blackmail photos ever," she declared.

"Oh, I'm pretty sure Papi destroyed them all. He may have destroyed the camera itself, just to be sure."

They laughed.

"If I go with the butt flap option, I should probably embroider something on it," Amber mused.

"For a good time, press here?" Carmen suggested.

Amber dissolved into giggles. "You're going to get me in so much trouble someday."

"You bet," Carmen agreed. "If your articles don't get it done, I've got your back. You can count on it."

They grinned at each other through the phone.

Cole

Cole sat at the picnic table in the woods behind Marin Henderson's house. The Coleman lantern and the pair of citronella candles cast a gentle glow against them. Just enough to see the outline of her shirtless form as he ran his hands up and down her bare skin, up over the bra strap, down into the waistline and back.

It wasn't their first time. It wasn't even their second. They liked each other, and while neither was really the going-steady type, they seemed to fall back into their rituals pretty easily every month or so. She'd been happy to take his call. She'd welcomed him to the yard with warm fingers, warm lips, and a willing smile. She was everything he wanted and needed tonight.

He sat on the bench with his back to the table. Marin straddled his lap, cupping his face in her hands and working her considerable magic on his mouth. When the time was right, he could lift her up and lay her on the tabletop, where she'd already spread out a soft cloth. It wasn't their first time.

Except . . . her magic wasn't working. The practiced kisses that usually took his mind off of anything were not working. Ugh.

He wasn't *in the mood*, Cole slowly realized, which was a literal first. And truly horrifying.

Horrifying was the name of the game tonight, all around. Marin's hot breath on him was making everything closer and more real, not pushing it into the distance.

"I want you," she whispered.

"I want you too," he said. But Emmy, in the car, had said that too. And after that the echoes kept reverberating.

You scared me, Emmy had said. That echo bounced around his mind, and it brought a friend. *It was terrifying,* his mom had said. The look on her face had spoken volumes.

Emmy: *We don't really know each other.*

His mom: *We didn't know each other that well, I didn't think.*

God damn it. The last thing Cole wanted to think about while he was making out was his mother. So freaking gross.

He pulled away from Marin. "I need to catch my breath," he said. He tugged her closer, wrapping his arms around her and holding tight. She lowered her mouth to his neck.

"I—I don't think we should do this tonight," Cole said.

"How come?" Marin whined. "It's not like we've never done it before."

Every answer he had to that question felt supremely unmanly. "Um. Teen pregnancy is on the rise, you know."

"Ew." Marin wrinkled her nose. "If I got pregnant, I'd definitely get an abortion. So there's nothing to worry about."

"That's easy to say in a vacuum," Cole said. "You don't really know what you'd do. Or if it would even be legal anywhere nearby at the time you needed it." After *Dobbs,* the Supreme Court case that overturned *Roe v. Wade,* Indiana had passed a state law prohibiting abortion.

"I'd go to Illinois," Marin said. "Babies are gross. And I don't want to get fat until I absolutely have to."

"Fat and pregnant are two different things," Cole said.

"Like red apples and green apples." Marin grinned. She leaned toward him again.

Normally this was what he liked about Marin. She was uncomplicated. An easy hookup. No muss, no fuss, no hundred hours of preamble.

I would want to talk a lot more, Emmy had said.

"I think I have to take a rain check," Cole admitted. "I have a lot on my mind. I'm distracted."

Marin frowned. "You called me. This is what we do. Isn't it what you wanted?" She reached over and started rubbing his thigh, moving upward.

Cole pushed her hand away. He didn't want it. He wanted to *talk,* God help him. He dropped his head into his hands. Who was he becoming?

"You know I date a lot of girls," he said. "Is that really okay with you?"

Marin pouted. "But you like me best of all. I'm the one you're taking to prom."

"That's true," he said. About prom, at least.

"Anyway, I'm not a puritan," she said. "We can have sex just to have it, not as this big symbol of our relationship."

Yes. This was what he was always saying. So why was he getting in his own way?

"Some stuff happened today," Cole admitted. "I don't even know what to say about it."

Marin petted his face. She petted his chest and then his thigh. "I can make you feel better about it, don't you think?" She leaned upward to kiss him.

"I said no," he repeated, and the words reverberated through his body and his mind.

I said no a lot of times, Emmy had said. *You weren't listening.*

Cole burst out crying. It wasn't the same thing. Not at all.

Marin couldn't pin him to the table and force him into anything. But the disconnect made him feel sad and alone and the immensity of that feeling set him off. He couldn't imagine what his mother had been through. It hurt to have the mythical father figure of his imagination be knocked from his pedestal so hard. He'd always hoped to learn that he was like his absent father. Now he feared that he was.

"Oh, Coley," Marin cooed. "What's wrong?"

"I fucked up," he admitted. "Everything is totally fucked."

Marin let him rest his head against her chest, petting his back while he cried. After a few minutes, he dried his eyes on his wrists. He was horrified at his outburst.

"I need to go home," he said. "I'm sorry. I have to think about some things."

"Aww." Marin pouted. "Okay. Well, don't think too long. Prom is coming up."

"I know," he said.

"You're going to love my dress," she promised. "We're going to have so much fun."

"We will," he agreed, kissing her gently. That was a near certainty, in as much as he'd ever be able to have fun again in his life. "I'll see you soon."

Blossom

Blossom leaned against Julio's chest. It felt good, being together and quiet.

"Sorry. This doesn't have to be the only thing we talk about."

Julio laced his fingers into hers. "It's weighing on you."

"Yeah, but we could just zone out and watch some videos for a while. Learn some new dance moves to show off at prom."

Julio laid his cheek against her hair. "Do you want to talk about what really scares you here?"

"What?" Her heart rate ticked up a notch.

"I don't think pregnancy is the biggest risk here. It's pretty unlikely, in this day and age, that if you're on the pill and I'm in a condom that you would get pregnant."

"I know," Blossom admitted. It was only one of the factors that went into being ready or not, but it was the one with the most significant consequences.

Julio spoke softly. "I'm more scared about what happens next."

"Next?" Blossom echoed.

His thumb brushed her palm. "I feel like at some point we made a decision to live in the moment and not worry about the future, but we never said it out loud."

He was right. He was so right that Blossom grew dizzy with it. She couldn't speak.

"We screamed with each other on FaceTime when you found

out. You were over at my house when I found out. We gorged on Thai food and cheesecake, respectively, to celebrate together. We've never been anything other than thrilled that we both got into our first-choice school." Julio took a deep breath. "But . . . what happens in the fall, when you go away to Harvard and I'm at NYU?"

They were still sitting side by side, but suddenly she could feel the miles and miles of space that would soon be between them.

"It's only a four-hour train," Blossom said. "I looked it up."

"I know. Me too."

"You did?" Blossom's chest and stomach flooded with relief. She breathed into the sudden and unexpected softening of her whole being.

"So how come we never talked about it?" Julio asked. "We could have been making each other feel better all this time."

Blossom thought about it. "I guess it's scary to be the one to say it? Because if you said you didn't want to stay together after the fall, we'd basically be breaking up right now."

"So we were both trying to delay the moment of truth?"

"Seems like it." Blossom slid her arms around his neck and smiled joyfully. "But you were brave." It was like a weight had been lifted. One she hadn't fully realized she was carrying.

"I think it's easy to say we're worried about pregnancy. That's reasonable, especially in this time and place, when reproductive rights are being eroded."

Blossom sat back. "Yeah, and it's infuriating to feel that way when I know the whole point of anti-choice legislation is to control women's bodies, to make it hard for us to choose pleasure without assuming the consequences of motherhood. They *want* me to be in this conundrum." She affected a mock-deep, condescending voice. "No playing it fast and loose, ladies. Beware!"

Julio chuckled at her impression. "I agree with all of that. But let's jump back off the soapbox for a minute."

Blossom closed her mouth sheepishly. "It's a reflex."

"Probably because you spend too much time with Amber."

They laughed. "I'mma tell her you said that."

"She'll be proud."

"No doubt."

Julio turned serious again. "It's easy to cite statistics. It's harder to trust that we won't hurt each other."

Blossom lowered her head. "I know you'd never hurt me."

"Not on purpose," Julio said. "Not meanly."

"I trust you. I might even let you see me naked, though you'll have to agree to the 'no photos' clause in advance."

Julio cringed. "Oh, god. Agreed. Immediately." He stared into the distance. "You know I would never pull shiz like that jerk Astin did last week, and blast your cup size to the whole world, or whatever."

"He's done way worse than that."

"I know, but I don't like talking about it," Julio admitted. "It feels like condoning his behavior to even speak about it."

"It's not like I don't know what happened. Literally the whole school saw Lulu Carmichael's asymmetrical boobs."

"I know."

"She had to go on medication to deal with the stress from all the comments and bullying after."

"I heard that too."

"Argggh," Blossom growled. "It's hard to believe Ratliff is more worried about what we wear to prom than she is about preventing things like that."

"He should've been expelled."

"Seriously. What does it matter if your prom dress is chaste as hell when the guy you hook up with after blasts naked pics to the whole world?"

"For real, though—you know I would never, right?"

"I do, but we still have to agree to no photos. I trust you, and I'm telling you I trust you, but I don't want to play any weird games about it."

Julio nodded. "You mean, like me saying 'if you really trusted me, you'd let me take a photo'?"

"Yeah. Promise you won't?"

"I promise." Julio frowned. "It never even occurred to me, honestly. And I think about your boobs a *lot*."

"Julio!" Blossom smacked him lightly on the arm.

He grinned. "Just being honest. Look, I think that's a bogus game. No one should ask you to prove you trust them by doing something that makes you uncomfortable. I can't even believe we have to worry about that."

"But we do. Especially girls."

"I get it," Julio said. "No photos. Cross my heart."

"Even when we're long-distance?" She was worried about something far off, but this conversation had brought it a bit closer. There were so many ways to screw things up. What if she tried to draw one line too many and he bailed?

Julio wrapped her in his arms again. "I promise never to do anything that makes you uncomfortable. All you have to do is tell me what you want."

"Okay."

He sighed. "There's so much weird pressure. Let's both promise to do what's best for us and ignore the noise."

Blossom lifted her head and met his gentle gaze. "Forget

the haters. Forget the legislators. Forget the gossip mill and the internet. Just you and me?"

"Signed," Julio asserted.

"Co-signed."

They sealed the deal with a kiss.

THEN

August 2005

Sheryl

Sheryl opened the door for Tana. "You didn't have to come all the way over here."

Silently Tana swept inside and made her way to the living room. Sheryl followed. Luckily, no one else was home at the moment. It had gotten pretty frustrating to keep hearing from her foster mom about what a mistake her whole life had become. Mrs. Jones might have been okay with Sheryl staying the summer, but staying indefinitely with a baby was "a different kettle of fish," to quote her foster mother. So Sheryl had to find a job and an apartment as soon as possible, and finish her course registration at the local college.

"What's going on?" Sheryl asked.

"Let's sit down," Tana said, perching on the edge of the saggy armchair.

"What?" Sheryl put her hands on her hips.

Tana pointed at the couch, again suggesting she sit. "Rob's father called me today with a new offer."

"I thought you told them to shove it."

"I did. I've told them a couple of times."

"So, it's a thing with them, to basically never listen." Sheryl tossed herself down on the couch and crossed her arms.

"It's a serious offer and I think you should consider it."

"I want him to pay for what he did. And I don't want it to happen to anyone else."

"There's more than one way to make him pay," Tana reminded her.

"Yeah, but isn't this what always happens?" Sheryl said. They'd talked about this ad nauseam. "The rich kid does bad, ends up buying his way out. I feel like I'm part of a bad system if I take a little bit of money to keep my mouth shut. And what, he goes off to college? Lives his life?"

"This isn't a little bit of money," Tana said.

"Not sure I want to hear the amount, if it's going to be hard to say no to."

Tana nodded. "To be fair, what this offer tells me is that they're more scared of your chances in court than they've admitted up until now."

Sheryl felt a surge of hope. "So I have a chance to actually win?"

"Whatever you want to do, I'll support you." Tana brushed her hair back. "I'll find you a great team of lawyers to support you, but in the end, it'll be a local prosecutor arguing the case against whatever big shot Mr. Clayton brings in for the defense."

Sheryl sat quietly. "I want real justice."

"Me too," Tana said. "But they're not playing around anymore. Sheryl, this is keep-the-baby, live-your-life money."

Sheryl took a deep breath. "How much are they offering?"

"Two million dollars."

Mina

Mina hauled the large suitcase up onto the foot of her bed. Once it was full, it'd be bigger than what she should probably lift, but she'd cross that bridge when she came to it.

Her mother stood in the doorway shaking her head. "You're not seriously leaving."

"Dad made my options pretty clear," Mina said. "Go to college or get cut off."

"You're not due till January. You could do a semester. It would be much easier to go back if you start rather than deferring."

"I'm going to have to get a job for the next few months, so I have something to live on when the baby comes."

"Your father's going to come around."

Mina made a face. "I doubt it." She'd lived with his my-way-or-the-highway attitude her entire life, and when push came to shove, she'd always caved to the pressure. Childhood tantrums, teen rebellion, all shut down because in the end she didn't want to hurt him. At this point she wasn't even sure if Harvard was an idea she'd come up with herself, or if it was yet another reflection of her father's vision. His butthurt I've-been-betrayed big-mood stomping around the house suggested the latter. He didn't know what it meant to not get his way. It was downright immature. Embarrassing even.

Mina threw clothes in the suitcase, trying to be somewhat judicious and not entirely random, though her hands were shaking. Baggy things, loose things—anything that had a chance of still fitting over the next few months, plus her general favorites that hopefully would fit again in the long term.

"It's scary to him, the idea of you going out in the world with a child to support. No education? How will you get a job good enough to support yourself? He's terrified."

Mina paused in front of the dresser, resting her hands on her jewelry box atop it for stability. Was her mother really suggesting that Mina have compassion for her father's fears about her future? What about *her* fears?

"Uh, I don't know, okay?" If it wasn't for Penney offering to take her in for a while, Mina didn't even know if she'd be able to go through with it. She'd have to throw herself on her parents' mercy, no doubt. She didn't have secret scrappy survival skills. She hated to so much as chip a nail. Nonetheless, she spun around to face her mother. "Why are you putting this all on me? Making it about me hurting Dad? This was all his idea to begin with. Remember that part?"

"Mina."

"What? He said it. He said the words. 'Get an abortion or you're no longer welcome under this roof.'"

"He didn't mean it."

"So why isn't he in here, telling me you'll support my choice?"

"We can't support you forever."

You could, if you wanted to, Mina thought. Her parents weren't hurting for money. The fight was idealistic, which made it all the more painful. It spoke volumes that the idea of supporting her, to them, meant solely taking care of everything financially.

"I'm not asking you for money. I'm getting out of your hair, see?" She gently placed the jewelry box into the suitcase. "I'll figure it out."

Mina refrained from saying that if it wasn't for Penney, she'd have to stay. She'd have to fight her way forward and hope her parents changed their mind. She'd have to get stubborn in her father's face and pray that he didn't drag her bodily to the door.

She didn't have a real plan. She didn't have resources. And since she'd always had her parents and their resources backing her up, the thought of being truly out in the cold was paralyzing.

Her mother crossed her arms. "Where are you going to live? You're going to need us to co-sign an apartment."

"Mom, lots of people get apartments without their parents."

"Not decent apartments."

Mina stared at her mother. "Yeah, it's probably not going to be up to your upper-middle-class standards. But I'll sleep on the street if I have to," she declared. That wasn't remotely true. She was weak and entitled and the thought of so much as sitting on the pavement under a bridge grossed her out hard.

"He's acting like it's three months ago and if he pouts hard enough, I'll change my mind and do things his way. But it's far too late, Mom. And I'm not five years old anymore, living for Dad's approval."

"Mina—"

"Please get out of my room," she said. "I need to be able to think in order to pack."

"But—"

"Mom." Mina took her by the shoulders and steered her toward the hallway.

"I really want—"

"The thing about cutting me off, Mom, is that I don't have to care what you want anymore."

Her mom's mouth dropped open.

Mina closed the door in her face.

Sheryl

Two million dollars. The number echoed in Sheryl's head, too large to find any place to rest. Tana had told her to sleep on it; she'd promised Mr. Clayton an answer by noon tomorrow.

Sheryl lay in bed. She slid her hand over her belly, still so flat-seeming when she was horizontal. It was hard to fathom the tiny life that lay within. She was surrounded by the unfathomable, and at some point she knew she'd have to make the choice to believe.

Two *million*? That was the amount you'd get for working two hundred thousand hours at a ten dollar per hour job. That was twenty-five thousand eight-hour shifts. Working 365 days a year, that equated to over sixty-eight years of work. And she'd be lucky to land much better than a ten dollar per hour job with only a high school diploma and a kid to care for full-time. Once she started college, she might get something that paid more, but it would have to be part-time, so she could study. Even with a full-time, twenty dollar per hour office job with weekends off, it would take forty-eight years to make that much money.

Or, she could take the settlement and breathe easy for the next fifty years. For the rest of her life, really, if she was careful.

Two million dollars.

Sheryl shivered. She was dealing with people who had two million dollars at their disposal. That was shocking. Terrifying.

Two million dollars would buy a lot of food and diapers. It was an insane amount of money. Completely absurd.

She knew in her heart that Tana was right: This offer meant Mr. Clayton had been bluffing about her chances in court. She could win.

Her hand drifted over her belly to the place she hadn't been able to touch in over a month. The place that had borne the brunt of Rob's aggression. The place that would soon enough bear her child. *I'm sorry*, she whispered.

Her body was no longer her own. Her decisions were no longer her own. She could feel the tiny life inside her, even though she hadn't felt the baby move yet. Science might say that was impossible. But it felt very real to her. Sheryl knew she had a choice, and she wouldn't begrudge someone else choosing different—in fact if you'd asked her six months ago, hypothetically, she'd have said *no way, for sure, that'd be a no-go, having a baby at eighteen*. She'd had plans.

Her chest ached. She pressed her hands against her breastbone, as if she could soothe her heart with a touch. She wanted to feel strong. She wanted to stand in Rob's face and say there was no amount of money that could make her step down from the pursuit of justice. She wanted to testify and, no matter the outcome, know that she had said her piece. She wanted to give all the college girls Rob was about to meet a caution to think twice.

She wanted to do what was right. But her world had changed. Her new reality put new demands on her.

She wanted to do what was right. So what was that?

Mina

Mina lay on her bed in the fetal position for a long while after packing. The wheels of her suitcase dug into her hip. She'd gathered most of what she was taking, but now she had stalled.

She didn't think her parents would gut her room immediately. She hoped there'd be time in the next few weeks to come back for a few things, if they let her. But she supposed there was a chance they wouldn't. So she made sure she had packed everything she truly and deeply cared about. In the end, she had her checked bag, her carry-on, a duffel and two backpacks, and three large plastic bins. She wondered if it was more or less than what she'd have had to pack to go off to college.

Mina dragged herself off the bed. She started rolling a suitcase toward the door. It was heavy. Uh-oh. What were the odds of her making it down the stairs with this? The carry-on bag wouldn't be much of a problem, but the checked bag was huge. And she couldn't ask her dad for help, like usual.

She reached over and dialed Penney. "I don't think I'm going to be able to get my suitcases down the stairs," she admitted. "So much for independence."

"If you don't wanna call baby daddy, I'll send Colby over," Penney promised. "No problem."

Mina groaned. "I can't call Chip. He's being so weird."

"Okay, I'll text Colby."

"How come he can be so normal and Chip can't?" Mina complained.

"Colby's not normal," Penney reminded her. "Any guy would wig out at being told they're gonna be a dad at eighteen."

"But Colby didn't."

"Oh, he did." Penney laughed. "He just knows how to pull up his socks. Like we did."

"I'm wearing anklets."

"It's a metaphor."

"I know . . ." Mina buried her face in her pillow. "I can't do this."

"There's always adoption," Penney said.

Mina lay quietly. "It isn't about the sanctity of life or whatever. That's not why I decided to have the baby."

"The point is, even if it's too late in one sense, it's not too late to change your mind about actually raising the kid."

"If I was going to be able to give her up, I don't think I'd have had a problem with an abortion," Mina said.

"That's two totally different things," Penney argued. "Adoption just means giving the kid a chance at a better life, if you think you can't do right by them."

"But you're not giving yours up."

"Nah," Penney said. "The kid could do way worse than having me for a mom."

"Me too," Mina said quietly. "At least, I think so." She wished she shared Penney's enthusiasm and confidence.

"Of course. So, what time do you want me and Colby to come by and get you?"

"I'm basically ready." As ready as she'd ever be, anyway. "So anytime is good."

"We'll be there in an hour."

"Thanks." Mina hung up, then curled herself up even tighter.

Sheryl

In the morning, Tana stood on the front porch again, looking far too glamorous for this neighborhood.

"It's hard to believe Rob's dad has two million dollars."

"He doesn't, entirely. The money would be paid out in approximately one-hundred-thousand-dollar installments over the next eighteen years."

Sheryl frowned. "But, that's longer than the statute of limitations. What if he stops paying once I can't change my mind and press charges?"

Tana smiled. "That's an incredibly smart question, babe. Once they sign, they'll be legally bound to pay you, just like you'll be legally bound to silence about the incident. If they stop paying, then you sue them for breach of contract."

"The statute of limitations is only seven years. That's a long time for him to screw me over."

"We could push for a lump sum payment, but I honestly believe this deal is better for you. No judge is going to support Jerk Junior signing away his parental rights without some indication of child support. An eighteen-year payout covers those bases and frees you from the possibility of a custody battle down the way."

"Custody battle?" Sheryl clutched at her stomach instinctively. "They didn't even want me to have the baby. You think he would want custody? How could that be?"

Tana shook her head. "I know, babe. It's a messed-up world where the guy who raped you could get custody of your child, but it's possible. Especially if he's acquitted in court. Then he's not your rapist, legally speaking. He's just the father of the baby, with all the rights and privileges that go along with that."

Sheryl nodded, the truth dawning on her. "He could take the baby."

"Yes, and a court might well grant him custody if it seems like he's better equipped financially to care for the baby and could provide a more stable home. Most judges won't rip a baby from a loving mother, but if Rob fights you for it, a shared custody situation is likely."

"He wouldn't."

"Probably not now. But in five years, or ten? When he's not headed off to frat life, and has a job and a house and family of his own? When he realizes a piece of his DNA is walking around outside of his control? When it comes to family, people like the Claytons do things you wouldn't expect."

Sheryl endured a flutter of panic. "How does the settlement stop that?"

"It's a system of mutual benefit. They're trusting you to drop the charges and not speak of Rob's actions, and never to approach him with demands related to paternity. In exchange, he'll sign away his parental rights, so he can never come back and try to take the baby. It's a clean break for everyone."

"I'm supposed to trust the guy who raped me?"

"Look, I know that it's a big decision. If what you really want is to tell the world what he did, and hopefully to see him behind bars, then you don't have to take the deal. But just know that his dad will spend that two million on legal support to get Rob cleared of the charges. He's pretty well-connected, so he might

208 | PROM BABIES

even find a way to get the DA to drop the charges. It enrages me to the sky and back that this is the world we live in, Sheryl, but money talks. You and your baby could be taken care of for the rest of your lives. That's a kind of justice, don't you think?

"If you have the baby and don't take the money, you'll be raising a child on your own. He'll no doubt dispute child support, and even if you win some in court, it would be a lot less than this."

Sheryl understood. "So, I live with it. Swallow the truth about what he did to me and go be a mom who doesn't have to work much?"

Tana took Sheryl's face in her hands. "That last bit sounds like a pretty good deal."

In the end, she knew she couldn't walk away. If there wasn't a baby, maybe she'd chase Rob through court. Maybe she'd take the stand and bravely tell the world what he did to her. But what if she couldn't? And if he was found innocent, she'd have nothing.

Mina

Colby and Penney rolled up in his Chevy Silverado, a gray pickup truck that looked like it had been around the block more than a few times.

Penney waved as they rolled into the driveway. "Hey, Meen," she called out the window. She seemed to be one of those people who wanted to nickname absolutely everyone immediately.

Mina waved back but stayed seated. Equilibrium was important at the moment. Her stomach seemed to be experiencing a surge of morning sickness. The second trimester was supposed to be better than the first on that front, but so far that had not been her experience. Plus, she seemed to be having hers in the afternoon too.

She had come to sit on the front porch to wait. A ringing doorbell would surely have brought one of her parents to the door, and Mina hoped to avoid any parental encounters for as long as possible during the move out.

Penney hopped out before Colby had even shut off the engine and strolled up the walkway to meet her. This was the first time, seeing her, that Mina could discern a slight change in her gait. As your hips shifted during pregnancy, it made you walk a little differently, Mina had learned from one of the books the three friends were sharing. She could feel that difference a little bit in herself now as she moved, her center of gravity slowly changing.

Penney bent down and hugged Mina where she sat on the wicker chair. "You all packed?"

"Packed and ready," she said, though the nausea roiling in her stomach couldn't entirely be attributed to morning sickness.

"Point me toward the heavy stuff," Colby said, leaping onto the porch as if to advertise his physical prowess.

"Just a sec." Mina scooted toward the edge of the chair and felt her stomach contents shift. "Erm . . ."

"You okay?" Penney asked, leaning a hand on her shoulder.

"I'm a little queasy," Mina admitted. "My morning sickness is more of an all-day sickness at this point."

"Just tell me which room, and I'll start grabbing stuff," Colby said.

"Top of the stairs, first bedroom on the right. The one with all the suitcases piled up on the rug."

"Got it," Colby said.

"Thanks," Mina said. "I could do it myself if I wasn't such a basket case."

"You did the right thing calling us," Penney said. "Colby needs the workout anyway."

"I didn't hear you complaining last night," he tossed over his shoulder.

Penney clicked her tongue at him. "We don't kiss and tell," she scolded.

Colby disappeared inside.

"You two are beyond cute," Mina commented.

Penney squeezed her knee. "I'm lucky," she said seriously. "And I do know it."

Mina nodded. She didn't want Chip in her life full-time, not the way Penney wanted Colby. But it would've been nice to feel less entirely alone.

Penney

Penney dialed up Sheryl first thing in the morning. "I've got Mina at my house now, and she could use some cheering up," Penney announced without preamble.

"What did you have in mind?" Sheryl asked.

"A little trip to the mall, for starters. Pick you up in an hour?"

"Is the mall even open yet?"

"We'll get breakfast on the way," Penney suggested. "We preggos need our fuel."

"I'm in," Sheryl said. "I could use a little cheering up myself."

"Something happen?" Penney asked.

Sheryl was quiet for a moment. "There's been a . . . development."

"I'm intrigued," Penney declared. "See you in an hour."

Penney borrowed her mom's car and she and Mina drove over to Sheryl's place to pick her up. They stopped for breakfast at the Bob Evans located right down the road from the mall. Cheap. Delicious. Perfect. They even ordered an extra stack of pancakes for the table, because if not now, when?

"Come on, now," Penney said as they headed into the mall. "First stop, perfume counter."

"I don't really wear perfume," Sheryl said.

"I have a bunch already," said Mina.

"Doesn't matter," Penney said. "This is our fresh start. Pick a scent you've never worn. Smell is the most powerful sense, you know. It relates hard-core to memory. If you smell different, you're like a new person."

"Just like that?" Sheryl asked.

"This is what my mom does every time she breaks up with someone. Get a new perfume. Something that makes you feel like you again. Or the you you want to be." Penney waved her hand. "It's flexible."

The three friends sniffed and sniffed various samples, spritz squares, and sprays. They sniffed until they practically felt lightheaded.

Mina chose an earthy, grounded mix made with sandalwood and cedar, with notes of smoky pine. Sheryl chose a light, floral jasmine-lily combo. And Penney picked a summery, full-bodied honeysuckle blend. They paid for the perfume and went out into the parking lot. Penney used the edge of her house key to open the plastic packaging on each box. They stood a few feet apart and liberally sprayed themselves with their new scents. A cleansing ritual.

"Like new," Penney said. It felt good.

The three young women smiled at each other. Then suddenly Sheryl's expression turned puzzled.

"What's wrong?" Mina asked. "Are you okay?"

"I felt something," Sheryl explained, pressing her hand against the side of her slightly protruding belly. "Oh, my god. There it is again. Quick!" She grabbed Mina's hand and pressed it against her side. Penney added her hand to the pile, symbolically. She'd felt her baby move for the first time a few days earlier. She'd been with Colby, which was amazing, but he hadn't been able to feel anything from the outside. Soon, she was sure. Very soon.

"That's wild," Sheryl breathed. She caught the scent of her new perfume in the process. Her face broke into a smile again.

"Baby Brewster approves!" Penney cheered.

Sheryl

Next, Penney took them out for milkshakes. They rolled up to a local burger joint and she ordered a shake for everyone and a plate of fries to share.

"Extra pancakes and now French fries and ice cream?" Mina groaned. "If I didn't know better, I'd think you were trying to fatten us up."

"Well, we can't have coffee and if there was ever a time to glory in the calories and not care about our waistlines, this is it."

"Speak for yourself," Sheryl said. "I never worry about my waistline."

"That's because you're naturally slender," Mina told her. "Some of us have to work at it."

"We're young!" Penney declared. "And somehow I doubt our looks are going to be our first priority for the next few years."

"Ugh," Mina said. "When you put it like that . . ." She scooped a liberal amount of ketchup onto a pair of fries and chowed down. "What I do have to think about," she added, "is finding a way to make money. I can't eat out twice a day and expect to be able to afford rent."

"Do you even have a job yet?" Penney asked.

"No," Mina said. "But I have a little savings. And a credit card."

Sheryl and Penney exchanged a concerned glance. "And your parents aren't cutting those off?"

Mina frowned. "Why? It's mine."

Sheryl felt a sharp stab of jealousy. This girl had no idea what it really meant to be out on your own. She was lucky. "Um. You do know that someone has to pay the credit card bill in the end, right?"

"Of course," Mina said. "But by the time I have to pay it I can have a job and be making my own money."

"What kind of job are you thinking of getting?" Penney asked.

"I don't know." Mina mused on it. "Retail, I guess. I'd be good at selling perfume, like the clerks we met at the mall." She glanced around the restaurant. "Or waiting tables. Then you at least make tips."

"Unless it's a pretty good restaurant, your base pay is crap, though. Two dollars and ten cents an hour."

"You don't make minimum wage as a waitress?" Mina looked shocked. "Isn't that illegal?"

Penney shook her head. "Different class of worker. It totally sucks." Penney had worked two nights a week as a diner waitress for the last two years. "And some people don't even tip, because they think it's extra."

"Oh, my god. What am I even going to do?" Mina buried her face in her hands.

"This is worse than we thought," Penney mumbled to Sheryl, who nodded.

"I'm going to have to move back home," Mina wailed. "Why did I think I could make it on my own?"

"Relax," Penney said. "You're staying with me for now. You have time to figure it out."

"You've been so nice, but I can't mooch off you forever."

"Not forever," Penney agreed. "Just till you figure yourself out."

"I'm afraid that could take forever," Mina quipped, dropping her face back into her hands.

"You can mooch for more than one night, though," Penney said. "Let's try not to be rash."

"I've already been rash!" Mina cried. "I. Moved. Out. Oh, god. Oh, god."

"I'm about to have some money," Sheryl blurted out, silencing the table. "I'm not allowed to talk about how much, or where it's coming from, but it's enough to rent a house that's big enough for all of us."

"You mean, like, live together?" Mina asked, surprised.

"You settled?" Penney asked at the same time, looking surprised as well, and disappointed. "I thought you were taking him to court."

"I'm not allowed to talk about it," Sheryl said. "I could get in big trouble."

Mina nodded. "It's okay."

"I'd have liked to see that asshole behind bars, but you gotta do what you gotta do," Penney said.

Sheryl pressed her hands together. "You can't both stay with Penney's mom forever, right? I don't have anyone to help me. We could help each other." It was a split-second idea, born of panic and fury, but it filled her with a powerful and deepening hope.

"If we work together, Penney can keep her job and finish high school. Mina and I can both enroll at the college part-time. Between us, there'll always be someone to watch the babies."

Mina shook her head. "You don't really even know me. Why would you want to help me?"

"Because it would help me too," Sheryl said. "I don't want to do this all alone, either."

Mina gazed at her skeptically. It was a generous offer. Too

generous to be believed, Sheryl realized. It would have felt that way to her if the shoe was on the other foot. But she meant it. She struggled to find words to explain.

"He took something from me," Sheryl whispered finally.

Penney reached out and gripped her hand.

"It makes me—" Sheryl shook her head and blinked back the tears. Now was the time to be strong, to be sure, to take charge. "Don't you see? I want to be the opposite of what he is. I don't just want to take something from him in return. I want to give something. That's how I make it better." Saying it out loud in those words helped crystallize the feeling of relief that overcame her at the thought of giving Mina a place to live. She had wanted to testify partly so she could help other women. But there was more than one way to be part of an empowered sisterhood.

Mina grasped Sheryl's other hand. "I need help," she said. "Maybe we both do."

"Maybe we all do," Penney tossed in. She held out her other hand to Mina, who accepted it, closing the circle.

"My parents will freak," Mina said, with a laugh. "I think they're still expecting me to change my mind and give the baby up for adoption or something."

"You don't have to care what they think anymore," Penney reminded her. "Remember?"

Mina closed her eyes. "It's totally whack, right? To have a baby at this age."

"Look who you're talking to," Sheryl said.

"I'm sure they'll come around." Penney put her arm around Mina. "Once there's an actual baby, and no turning back."

"Or maybe they won't." Mina's voice seemed small. Sheryl could tell that despite her bravado, left to her own devices she'd probably end up moving back home and caving to her parents' wishes.

"We're making our own choices now," Penney asserted.

Sheryl squeezed her hand. "And stronger for it. None of us asked for this, but we can do it. Together."

Mina nodded. "Okay. Let's do it."

"Can we look for a place near my mom?" Penney asked.

And just like that, it became real.

NOW

March 2024

Amber

Carmen sashayed up alongside Amber's locker. "How does it feel being the talk of the town all over again?"

"The new article's a total hit." Amber grinned enthusiastically. "Everyone's reading it."

"I know. That's what I just said."

Amber leaned forward and kissed her. "And I'm saying it again, because it feels good."

"Everyone's talking about how messed up the dress code is, and the First Amendment implications and everything."

"As they should be."

"I even heard some people talking about organizing a boycott."

Amber slammed her locker. "I don't want to boycott prom. That would punish us more than the powers that be."

"Aww, look who's secretly excited about prom." Carmen grinned. "A few days ago you were acting like going was the punishment."

Amber slugged her lightly. "Shut up. A girl can change."

Carmen was still amused. "What about anti-prom? I've heard of some schools organizing if they don't allow queer couples to attend as couples."

"Too much work. And we're allowed to go, so I want to."

Carmen shrugged. "Fair enough."

"I did have an idea, though. What if we all submitted our approved dresses but then show up in something else completely?"

"They'd probably deny us admission at the door."

"If *everyone* did it? It's not like there'll be bouncers."

"Two problems. One, everyone has bought their dress by now. Who's going to buy a second?" Carmen said. "And two, we'd never convince everyone to wear inappropriate clothing. Not everyone's as lascivious as me."

"Oooh." Amber sidled closer. "It sounds so sexy when you say it like that."

Carmen pressed her lips against Amber's ear and whispered, "Lascivious."

Amber shivered. "Yes. You know how I love a good vocabulary word. But not in public, baby. Save it for later."

"Actually, my lascivious nature is giving me an idea." Carmen tapped her lips thoughtfully.

"Stahp."

"Lascivious!" Carmen kissed Amber's cheek. Both were laughing. "I'm being legit, though. I like to show the girls, right? So I've learned how to do it without getting sent home every day. Dress codes aren't only a prom thing around here."

"Yeah. So?"

"So . . . what if we played within the dress code?"

"Where's the fun in that?"

"You're seeing my boobs right now, aren't you?"

"You bet I am." Amber craned forward to get a better view.

Carmen breathed deep and pulled her shoulders back, leaning into it. "See, there's the letter of the law, and the spirit of the law."

"Meaning?"

"The list of dress code rules is full of the spirit of the law. If you look at what it actually says, there's some assumptions being made. One significant assumption in particular. Which means—"

Amber caught on. "We can break the spirit of the law while following the letter?"

"Precisely." Carmen grinned. "We're just going to need a little help from our friends of the tuxedo persuasion."

BUFORD HIGH SCHOOL PROM DRESS CODE

YOUNG MEN
Tuxedo (black or other color)
—Tuxedos should include: bow tie or necktie, vest or cummerbund, dress shirt, jacket, and optional accessories such as suspenders or cuff links
—Shoes and matching socks (black or white/ivory)

YOUNG WOMEN
Formal evening gown (full-length)
Dressy cocktail dress (appropriate length)
Dress shoes or sandals

NOT PERMITTED
Jeans, cargos, sneakers, flip-flops, Crocs, ball caps, athletic gear

NO ONE WILL BE ALLOWED ADMITTANCE IF THEY DO NOT FOLLOW THE DRESS CODE.
Young women are required to submit a photo of themselves in their chosen dress to the main office for preapproval.

Blossom

"If there was ever a night to allow extended curfew, it's prom night," Blossom argued. She pushed the salt and pepper shakers around in a circle on the kitchen counter, studiously ignoring Mina's gaze.

"If there was ever a night I was most worried about you having an extended curfew, it's prom night."

"Point, counterpoint," Blossom muttered. "Just because you got pregnant on prom night, doesn't mean I'm going to."

"Let's all hope not."

Blossom amended her argument. "What I mean is, just because you had sex on prom night, doesn't mean I'm going to."

Mina's eyes narrowed. "Say more about that."

"No thanks," Blossom said. "Next."

"Have you started taking your pill yet?"

Blossom hesitated. "Yes," she confessed. The talk with Julio about the future had loosened something in her.

"I've already said you can push your usual curfew from eleven to midnight. Maybe you should quit while you're ahead."

"So you're choosing this moment to get all high and mighty with me?" Blossom confirmed.

"My way or the highway," Mina declared.

Blossom smirked. "Sounds right."

Mina's expression turned serious. "You know I'm kidding when I say things like that, right?"

"Sure," Blossom said.

"I want you to make your own choices. Plan your own life."

Blossom beamed. "So . . . I can stay out as late as I want?"

"Nice try." Mina smiled too. "The dance ends at ten. Home by midnight."

Blossom made a puppy-dog face. "But what about the after-party? A bunch of people are going cosmic bowling. A big group. You always say groups are good."

Mina stared at her daughter pointedly. "Are *you* going cosmic bowling with the big group?"

Blossom sighed.

"Tell me about your plans with Julio."

Blossom grunted in annoyance. Her mother had seen right through her ruse.

"You want to be trusted to stay out as late as you want? The price is honesty."

"Is staying out as late as I want actually on the table?" Blossom perked up.

Mina hesitated. "Yes."

"I don't know if I'm ready to have sex with him, if that's what you're asking," Blossom said. "But I do want to spend time with him. Is that so wrong?"

"No, hon. I just know how easy it is when you're young to make an in-the-moment decision that has lifelong consequences. No take backs."

"Mom, I get it."

"You can't totally get it. Your frontal lobe isn't fully developed yet."

God, if Blossom had to hear about her frontal lobe one more time . . . "Mom, please. You decided not to be a doctor, so you can't throw weird medical terminology at me."

"I read *Scientific American*," Mina said. "The frontal lobe thing is common knowledge."

"Look, I'm a good kid," Blossom reminded her mother. "I got into Harvard, remember? I'm going to go happily along to the Ivy of my dreams, just like you always wanted."

"I hope you're not doing it for me," Mina said.

"What?" Blossom asked.

"Going to Harvard."

"What are you talking about? It's our dream. Me in Harvard undergrad, you in Harvard law. You're going to apply in the fall and you're going to get in. And next year, you'll come join me in Boston." It was their grand plan. It had been for years. Since before she was born, even. "Isn't there a picture of me in a Harvard onesie?"

"That was Grandpa's doing," Mina said. "The brainwashing starts early."

"Huh?" Blossom knew there was some tension between her mom and her grandfather, but she had never totally known what it was about.

"I want to go to Harvard *now*," Mina clarified. "The truth is, back then, I didn't want to go to Harvard."

"What?" Blossom gasped. "What are you even talking about? It was either me or Kenyon-then-Harvard, and you chose meeee." Blossom batted her eyes.

"I got accepted to Kenyon. I thought that life path was what I wanted. But it wasn't." Mina gazed into her tea mug.

Blossom plopped down on the couch next to her mother. Something significant was happening in her mind, Blossom could tell. "Start from the beginning. You lost me."

"I figured it out years later. One night, watching you sleep. You were about four, and we'd had the worst day. You cried about everything. The oatmeal was too mushy. The banana was too firm. I had to wrestle you into your clothes. I yelled at you all day long. My patience was on thin ice already and then we broke a vase."

Blossom had a vague memory of running through the hallway, hearing the crash, and finding herself screaming amid a pool of water and glass shards.

"I think I remember that," she said. "Was it a really tall greenish vase, on the table in the hallway at Sheryl's?"

"Yeah, we still lived at Sheryl's then. They were flowers left over from Penney and Colby's wedding. Normally we wouldn't have had something that fragile around. That was the year Cole insisted on climbing and jumping off all the furniture all the time."

"He was a terror," Blossom remembered. "Thank god he found boy friends in kindergarten that he could wrestle and fight with instead of me."

Mina shook her head, returning to the story. "The vase was the last straw. We basically both spent the rest of the night crying until you fell asleep. And then I still had some of the vase mess left to clean up. It was one of those days where at the end of it you lie down and vaguely wish to die in your sleep so you don't have to get up in the morning."

"Mm-hmm," Blossom said.

"And I stood in the doorway, watching you sleep. And I had this thought like, if I'd never had you, I'd be in my first year of medical school by now."

"And you regretted that you weren't there?"

"The funny thing was, I didn't." Mina shook her head. "To be clear, I was one hundred percent miserable at that moment. I desperately wanted my life to be different. But I didn't want to rewind. I didn't want to be on that other track; I didn't want to jump to that particular parallel universe. I wanted something entirely different."

"What did you want?" Blossom asked.

"I didn't even know." Mina was quiet for a moment. "The point is, I think being pregnant was a relief, in a weird way. It gave me a concrete way to stand up to my parents."

"That's messed up."

Mina nodded. "I should have been brave enough to do it on my own, but I wasn't."

"You could have decided not to be a doctor, but still gone to college. I mean, that is what you ended up doing."

Mina nodded. "Back then, it all seemed part and parcel. Kenyon, Harvard, med school, doctor, house, car, marriage, kids. Like I was standing on a conveyor belt."

"Why are you telling me all this?"

"Because I want you to be free. I want you to go to Harvard because you want to, not because you think it's what I want for you."

"College doesn't feel like a conveyor belt to me."

"Okay," Mina said.

"It feels like a fun place to learn and meet people. And be in a big city. It's not like going to college guarantees you a job anymore." There were stories in the local newspaper all the time about how kids were graduating from college and moving back to town because there was nowhere else to go. "I don't even know what I want to be," Blossom added. "So, it's an adventure, right? A way to explore."

"It's all of those things," Mina agreed.

Blossom shivered with excitement at the thought of her upcoming adventures. She pictured herself walking across the quad, studying under a tree, taking in all the culture of the city with her new cool friends. Only one thing was missing from the snapshot.

"Mom . . ." Blossom hesitated, then pushed forward. Putting things out in the open made her anxiety better, she was learning. Fewer assumptions led to less stress. That was as big of an "aha" thunderbolt as Blossom had ever experienced. "Mom, do you think there are guys who really stick around? Or is love always ephemeral?"

Mina was quiet for a long moment. "Oh, honey."

"I mean—" Blossom didn't know how else to say it. "Even with a kid on the way, Dad didn't stay."

"Bloss." Mina shook her head, pressed her fingers to her lips.

"You have a different boyfriend every year now."

"That's because I get lonely. It's nice to connect with someone every now and then."

"They never last, though. Isn't that upsetting?"

Mina sighed. "Some of them want to," she admitted. "But I'm holding out for something that feels really right. A connection that isn't based on status or driven by the social expectation that we pair up as fast as possible or we've failed." She looked at the ceiling. "I want someone who's really good for me. For us. Someone who adds more than they take away. That's rare."

"I think Julio's rare."

"Very," Mina said. "If I thought he was bad for you, these convos would go differently." She took Blossom's hand. "In the end it's your life. Your body. Your heart. No one can tell you what's worth the risk except you."

Blossom nodded. "I've done a lot of research. I think we can be safe."

Mina stroked her arm. "That's not the risk I meant, baby. And I think you know that."

Amber

Amber burst through the front door at Mina and Blossom's house, shouting. "Bloss! Hey, B, you're not going to believe—"

Blossom and Mina were sitting on the living room couch. Amber drew up short. "Oh, hey."

"Hey," Blossom said. "Who lit your tail on fire?"

"The patriarchy," Amber declared. "As per usual."

"Sounds right."

"Mina, can I borrow this girl for a minute?" Amber gushed. "I'm really here to see Cole, but I could use a quick word."

"Sure," Mina said. "Do you want to stay for dinner after? I'm thinking pizza."

"Only if there's pineapple."

"Coming right up."

Blossom leaned over and hugged her mom, then hauled herself to her feet. "Really here to see Cole, you say? Why am I always the third egg in this sandwich?" she grumbled good-naturedly, following Amber upstairs to her bedroom.

When the door closed behind them, Amber let loose. "Carmen had a genius idea, Bloss. GENIUS. We have to get everyone to do it. It's the perfect dress code protest. It's gonna be epic."

"Everything is epic with you lately," Blossom noted.

"Okay, what's more epic than epic, then? This is going to be that."

Amber proceeded to outline the plan, and by the time she was through, Blossom was clapping her hands in excitement.

Cole

Cole nodded his head in agreement as Amber went over her plan. "Yeah, I can do that."

"Do you think your friends will do it?" She looked desperately hopeful. They were still standing in the entryway to his house because she hadn't even been able to hold her gush of thoughts in long enough to get farther inside.

"My friends? Sure," he said. "Not sure about literally every guy in the senior class, though."

"Can't you convince them?" Amber pleaded. "There's strength in numbers. The more the merrier." Carmen's brilliant protest plan would only work if a good number of seniors were willing to participate.

"Who do you think I am, some kind of pied piper?" Cole laughed. "I said, I'll spread the word. And share the link for those who might want to buy the . . . special garment."

"Thank you!" Amber exclaimed, tossing her arms around his neck. "You're the very best. I owe you one."

"Nah, it'll be fun. You have no idea how many of us have been called on Ratliff's carpet for some absurd reason or another. It'll be an honor to watch her eyes bug out of her head."

Amber laughed and picked up her book bag. "I'm going back over to Blossom's for a minute," she informed him. "They're getting pizza. You can come too, if you promise to leave some slices for the rest of us."

Cole tapped her arm. "Hey, before you go, can I talk to you for a second?"

"Sure."

"I mean, it's about a real thing. Can you not make fun of me for a minute about this?"

"Yeah, I can be real. You know that," Amber said. "I only joke because I love." She grinned and made a heart with her hands over her chest.

"Never mind." Of course she'd turn it into a joke. Amber made a face. "What? Why? That doesn't count as making fun of you. I swear, I can be serious."

Cole waved his hand. "Don't worry about it." He shouldn't drag her into this anyway. It was his own issue to deal with.

Amber dropped the goofy expression and lighthearted tone. "Hang on. You're really upset. What is it?"

Cole hesitated. He looked over his shoulder into the living room, as though checking to be sure they were alone. They were. His mom had been out all afternoon.

Finally he spoke. "You know how you always call me a dog?"

"Sure . . ."

"That's like, a real thing, right? You're not just giving me a hard time?" Cole said. "You think I'm a bad guy."

Amber frowned. "I don't think you're a bad guy."

"But you're also, like, not joking when you say 'don't be such a dog.'"

"No, I'm not." Amber dropped her backpack and sat down on the stairs, tugging Cole's arm to bring him along with her.

He settled onto the step above her and dropped his head into his hands. "I'm kinda getting that now."

Amber was silent for a moment. "What did you think it meant? Like, before now?"

"I thought you were just ribbing me. Like a sister. The way girls always make fun of guys for behaving like asses."

"Sometimes you're asses," Amber said quietly. "That feels very real to us."

"But not, like, all in fun?"

"Sometimes it's that too, but there's a line."

"I don't understand where the line is. I mean, I've heard about the line before, but I never thought that much about it, honestly. I didn't think it was a thing I really had to worry about."

"We all have to worry about crossing the line. And not hurting people."

"I know that now."

"What is this about? Did something happen?"

Cole hung his head. "I can't talk about all of it." If there was anyone he could trust, it was Amber. She was a hothead, but she wasn't going to blab. But, it was his mom's secret as much as it was his own.

"What's the part you can talk about?" Amber asked.

"Do you think I'm the kind of guy who could rape someone?" he blurted out.

Amber pulled back physically. "Whoa. Um. I mean—" She paused, thinking. "I don't think there's a 'type of guy,' per se. It's not an identity, it's an action. It's a behavior."

"No, but I feel like there's a type of guy who is that type of guy, right? The kind who inherently doesn't respect women. Or who treats them badly, or who is always a jerk to them. The rich white frat boy party type who feels super entitled."

Amber raised her eyebrows. "That's an oversimplification."

"But you know what I mean, right?"

"Sort of." Amber tapped her lip. "I think that type of guy is shown on TV a lot as a stereotypical Jerk You Don't Want to Date. A stock character."

"Yeah, that guy," Cole said. He could watch a cheesy romance alongside the women in his family and recognize the "bad" boyfriend that the heroine starts out the movie dating. It was usually easy to see why he was the wrong type.

"In real life it's more complicated." Amber chewed her lip, the way she did before she was about to dispense some truth.

Cole braced himself. "Just say it."

"It's interesting how you listed a bunch of qualities that feel 'other' to you. 'Entitled jerk rich white frat boy party type' or something like that?"

"Yeah."

Amber proceeded gently. "Look, you know I love you. But I've seen you with the women you date, or the ones you try to go after. You can be kind of a jerk. And definitely entitled. The party type goes without saying." She tipped her head down to stare at him over her glasses.

Cole felt a prickle at the back of his eyes. "So I am. You think I'm one of those guys."

Amber sighed. "I want to change your way of thinking about it."

"What do you mean?"

"I mean, all you have to do to not be 'the type of guy who could rape someone' is to proceed with gentleness when you interact with the people you date. Like, literally, just . . . don't rape anyone."

Cole frowned. "But, I wouldn't. Of course I wouldn't, but—"

"But you're here asking me if you could. So . . . ?"

Cole shook his head. He didn't have the words to explain how he was feeling.

Amber continued. "I get that you want to think of yourself as a good guy, and to have that be like a protective coat. You're a 'good guy,' so by extension you always have good intentions, so by extension you couldn't possibly do something awful."

"That would be nice."

"That's what I hear you asking me, though. If you're a good guy or a bad guy. Like it's a binary. Like it's a foregone conclusion. Like it doesn't have to do with how you act."

"I'm trying to make sure that I'm not that kind of guy."

Amber rubbed her forehead. "There's nothing I can say that will make you magically incapable of hurting someone."

"How am I supposed to ever hook up with a girl, if I can't tell whether I'm pushing too far?"

Amber stuck out her pointer finger firmly. "That's a completely separate issue. That's about listening. And communication. And erring on the side of NOT when you're not sure."

"Err on the side of NOT," Cole echoed.

"If you're not one hundred percent sure she's into it, pull back. Easy."

"It's not that easy."

"Yeah, it is. The rule is simple. Following it might not be, depending on the situation. That's where you have to be strong. And not selfish."

"Pull back."

"Look, you know how Blossom and I are always talking about systemic racism, and how the culture we live in is steeped in it? We all have these influences, these biases?"

"Yeah. I kind of have a handle on that."

"You're still a white boy, so keep on learning," Amber quipped. "But my point for the moment is that systemic misogyny is like that too."

"Okay."

236 | PROM BABIES

"Misogyny says 'guys want it; girls don't.' It says 'guys aren't manly unless they go for it and girls are slutty and loose if they do it.' That creates a lot of tension. For everyone."

"Girls sometimes act like they don't want it when they do, because they think they're not supposed to want it?"

"Maybe," Amber said. "But the bigger problem is guys *thinking* we do that—*thinking* that we secretly want it and not respecting our 'no.'"

I said no a lot of times and you didn't listen, Emmy had said.

"I know that no means no," Cole said. "Obviously." So why wasn't that what he had done in the moment? Where was the disconnect? In his own mind?

"Girls like to get it on too. When we're ready, we're as into it as guys are. When we're ready, you'll know because we'll tell you. In any situation where one person isn't willing or able to tell the other person point-blank that they're ready and want it . . . well, you probably shouldn't be having sex in that scenario."

"I guess that makes sense."

"You guess?" Amber sighed. "Misogyny is what makes guys think they'll never get any if they don't push hard for it in the first place. We're culturally trained to believe that guys always want sex, but girls have to be convinced. And some guys take that way too far."

"You sound like an after-school special."

Amber rolled her eyes and mock swooned. "I've always dreamed of a guy saying that to me. Finally, someone gets me," she added dryly.

"I don't even know why I'm asking you for girl advice," Cole admitted.

"Because you know I'll give it to you straight."

Cole smirked. "I thought you didn't give anything straight."

Amber grinned. "Touché, basshole. I'm over here trying to have a serious conversation, at your request, I might add, and there you go slammin' on me." She slung her arm around his shoulders, tugged his head down, and noogied it hard.

Cole yelped. "Hey. Failure to get consent! Failure to get consent!"

Amber shoved him away. "I'm like your sister. The rules are different. We have a shared understanding after many years of tussling. Seriously—I did that because I knew it wouldn't offend you, not really. Plus, I can beat your ass without regrets and we both know it."

"So what you just did . . . I can do that to you and Blossom, but not a girl who's a friend."

"Probably, yeah. You do need consent if you want to touch someone who isn't family."

"So, anytime I want to kiss a girl, I have to ask first? Like literally say 'Can I kiss you now?'"

"Um, yes. Yes, that is exactly what you should do."

"Doesn't that take away all the spontaneity and romance?"

"For some people, consent itself is romantic." Amber knocked on his temple. "Try to get that through your thick head. Until you know someone well enough to be sure she likes getting taken off guard, better to play it safe." She chucked his arm. "That's what a good guy would do, anyway."

Cole sighed.

"Confused or clarified?" Amber asked.

"Somehow, kind of both?" Cole admitted. He stared at the closed front door. "There's a lot of stuff I don't know what to think about."

"Did something happen?" Amber said softly. "This conversation has me wondering, what makes a leopard want to change his spots?"

"That's the part I can't talk about," Cole said.

Amber's knee nudged his. "People make mistakes. I still love you even if you made a mistake. You can tell me."

"That's not it, really." Cole fell quiet.

"That's good, then?" Amber suggested.

"I mean, I'm worried about some things I've done, but not that bad of stuff." *There's someone I need to apologize to*, he thought. But he couldn't admit it out loud and have Amber think less of him. He hadn't raped Emmy. He knew that. But he had pushed too hard and he was growing less and less comfortable each time he thought about their night in the back seat.

THEN
December 2005

Mina

Mina sipped a mug of hot chocolate and surveyed her tinsel stylings. Tinsel wasn't ever a thing at her childhood home, so she wasn't sure if she'd handled it right. Sheryl was upstairs, studying for her last final of the semester tomorrow, and Mina and Penney had decided to surprise her with decorations all done when she came downstairs for dinner. Colby had carried in the tree and now was seated on the floor beside her, untangling the string of new lights.

Mina rubbed her massive belly. The baby girl inside twirled. Perhaps she was reacting to the warmth of the cocoa. Perhaps she was dancing to the light Christmas music mix Penney had put on in the background. Her girl definitely loved to dance, Mina knew.

"Baby's first Christmas," Penney declared, coming up beside Mina. "She is feeling the music, I think. She's been lurching around all afternoon. I'm getting sore from it." She rubbed her sides.

"You okay?" Mina asked. Their due dates weren't identical, which was kind of funny, but they were due in mid-January. Only a few weeks to go.

"Yeah, just a little achy," Penney said. "Probably tired too."

Penney had pounded her final semester of high school extra hard in order to earn the credits to graduate without doing spring semester. Mina had finished her last essay final the night before and turned it in that morning. Now she and Sheryl both

242 | PROM BABIES

would be taking the semester off from the local college where they were enrolled.

Sheryl's settlement was gifting them all with a freedom they hadn't expected. Mina had worked as a seasonal employee at the local bookstore this fall, mostly wrapping gifts and occasionally staffing the coffee counter. The manager liked her, and she thought it was likely they'd hire her back for a part-time gig once the baby was a few months old. Penney still had her waitress job, but she'd be taking time off for the baby as well.

The doorbell rang. Penney looked preoccupied, so Mina waddled over to answer it. Her mouth opened in surprise. "Mom?"

Mina's mother stood on the porch, holding a festive gift bag and a box with a Christmas bow. "Hi," she said. Her eyes widened as they dropped to Mina's belly.

"Hi," Mina answered. Should she invite her in? Her parents had been standoffish with her all through the fall, and Mina wasn't sure what to make of this visit.

"I wanted to bring you your Christmas presents," Mom said, adding quietly, "and to see where you live?"

"Oh, okay. Thanks." Mina opened the door wider. Her mom stepped inside. She crossed over and laid the presents down under the newly erected tree. As she looked around the room, she seemed transparently surprised at the homey look of the place. It had looked rather sparse just a few hours ago, and Mina was suddenly grateful for Penney's nesting instincts.

Mina introduced her to Penney and Colby, who greeted her politely.

"And Chip?" Mom asked.

Mina shrugged. "I have friends, Mom. I don't need him." Chip was nowhere to be seen. She imagined he'd come home for Christmas like Colby, but so far he'd shown no interest in her pregnancy or the child they would soon share. Sheryl's lawyer friend, Tana, had assured Mina that she could help her secure child support when the time came.

Her mother nodded, her expression closing. "Well, I just wanted to see you." She reached out her hand, as though to touch Mina's belly, but at the last second, she pulled back. "You look so beautiful." She tucked her purse over her shoulder and moved toward the door. "Merry Christmas, sweetheart."

I don't need him, Mina had said. But maybe her mother had heard *I don't need you*. She didn't know how to walk it back. Her mom walked out the door and closed it behind her.

Penney put her arm around Mina. "That was huge," she said. "Huge."

Mina leaned on her friend. "You think?"

"Oh, yeah," Penney said. "They're going to come around. They're gonna take one look at their grandbaby and be the most doting grandparents you ever heard of."

Secretly, Mina hoped so.

"Now," Colby said. "Did I hear tell of some cinnamon cookies?"

Mina smiled. Yes. The dough was already chilling. Baking would be the perfect distraction. She smiled at her friends. "Coming right up."

As she headed toward the kitchen, she felt a sense of relief. Family was complicated. But these friends? They took each other as they were. And it was working. The strange little life they were building together was a gift, a miracle, like the babies themselves.

Sheryl

Sheryl closed her psychology textbook and laid down her pencil. Enough. She'd pass the test or she wouldn't, but her brain wasn't absorbing much more information at this point. She stretched and hauled herself awkwardly up from the desk. Maneuvering this belly was no joke. Of the three of them, she was the smallest—they'd measured, of course—and she could NOT imagine how it would feel to be any bigger.

She opened her bedroom door to the tinkling sound of "Jingle Bells" and the scent of cinnamon cookies wafting up from below. One more exam, and then she'd be able to join the holiday merriment wholeheartedly. But there was no harm in getting a little taste . . .

Sheryl descended the stairs into a veritable Christmas wonderland. A lit tree, complete with tinsel and ornaments. Candles and garlands everywhere. A random Santascape filled the fireplace mantel: a North Pole environment complete with reindeer taking off above a sleigh. Christmas place mats on the dining table. A centerpiece on the coffee table too. They didn't have much more furniture yet, but if they did it would likely have been festooned as well.

Colby and Penney were canoodling on the couch under a blanket shaped like a snowflake. He'd arrived home from college for the holiday break last night. Today he'd been helping Penney move her things in. She'd been living at home to finish out high school, but now that they were a few weeks from due, she'd begun to make the transition.

Sheryl joined Mina in the kitchen. She was bent in front of the oven, peering through the glass at the tray of baking cookies.

"Sheryl!" Mina smiled. "Just in time to taste test the first batch with me." She pulled on an oven mitt and lifted the tray out onto the stovetop. "They're supposed to cool for a few minutes, but I say we be rebels." She tapped a soft cookie off the side of the sheet onto a paper towel and held it out to Sheryl.

Sheryl broke off a piece, blew on it, and popped it into her mouth. It was a buttery, cinnamon-sugar dough that melted on her tongue. "Delicious," she declared.

Mina beamed.

From the living room, Penney and Colby squealed with laughter. Mina and Sheryl smiled at each other. Often this fall, it had been just the two of them here, and quiet. But the house really came alive when Penney was there.

"Let's get the lovebirds some cookies," Sheryl suggested. She pulled a plate from the cabinet and held it while Mina filled it up.

They carried the treats into the living room and joined the others. They dimmed the lights and sat together under the soft, festive music, regarding the lit, decorated tree.

This place felt like hers, Sheryl realized. Really and truly. The over-the-top lights and decorations represented something mythical, a sense of celebration that had only ever existed in her imagination up until now. She couldn't remember the last time she'd been surrounded by the trappings of Christmas to this degree. She couldn't remember the last time she'd felt this much at home.

They enjoyed a pleasant dinner of chicken and vegetables, cooked by Colby. Penney had promised that they could all expect a fair bit of spoiling while he was in town. Guilt about being away at college like a normal eighteen-year-old had him sending Penney small cards and gifts practically weekly. Whenever he came home for a weekend, he treated the girls to his considerable skills at home cooking.

They laughed and ate and then settled in to watch a cheesy Christmas movie. The opening credits had only just rolled, when Penney sat up. "Oh, no," she cried. "What the what?"

Colby hopped to attention. "What? What is it? What's wrong?"

"I feel funny," Penney said. "I've been feeling funny for a while, come to think of it." She glanced uncertainly at Mina and Sheryl. "I think I might be in labor?"

"It's too early to be in labor," Colby exclaimed in alarm. "You're not due for weeks!"

"Less than three weeks," Mina corrected. "That's pretty well within the normal range."

"I need to move," Penney said urgently. "I need to move."

Colby helped her to her feet.

"Uh-oh."

They all watched as Penney's sweatpants grew dark and damp.

"That would be your water breaking, I think," Sheryl said.

"Oh, my god," Penney said. "It's not even Christmas. I haven't even finished my shopping."

"Oh, my god," Colby said. "I have to get you to the hospital."

Penney reached toward Mina and Sheryl. "It's happening."

They took her hands. "You've got this," Mina whispered.

"A hundred percent," Sheryl said. She rushed to get Penney's go bag from the front hall closet and thrust it at Colby. Luckily they had packed the bags a week ago, on advice from their favorite pregnancy blog. "Take care of our girl," she said, as they hustled out the door.

Penney

The last twenty-four hours had been hellacious and amazing. It was all a bit of a blur.

Colby sat by her bedside, stroking her hand. "I'm glad it happened while I was home for the holidays," he said. "As nervous as I was driving you here from Sheryl's house, I would have been a wreck trying to get all the way back from West Lafayette in time for the birth."

"Our early girl." Penney smiled. "She must have really wanted to meet you."

"And we get to spend the first week of her life actually all together," Colby said. "That's a gift."

"It is," Penney agreed. "By the way, you can change all the diapers this week." She smiled innocently.

"Done," he said. "These are the easy baby poops anyway. I'm getting off light."

Penney laughed. "How do you even know that?"

Colby looked offended. "What? I never had to change my brothers' diapers, but I have little cousins. I've babysat a time or two."

"'A time or two'?" Penney echoed. "Geez, I really should have checked your references before committing to procreate with you."

"I have excellent references," he said. "I'm very reliable."

Penney felt a trill of nervous hope. He'd been great so far, but what if this was the easy part? What if he met someone else, amid the fanciness of the big university? Someone smart and worldly, and not stuck raising a kid back in his hometown.

"I hope so," she said, holding on to his fingers.

"Hey," he said, squeezing back. "You know I don't *want* to go, right? I'm doing it because getting my degree is what's best for all of us."

"I know." She tried to believe it. "You'll be back."

"Yeah. As often as I can." He touched her cheek. "You know I'm gonna marry you, right?"

Penney's heart stilled. "Are you proposing?" It was still no guarantee, but it was a lot more than nothing.

"No," he said. "But I'm gonna. When you're not, you know . . ." He waved his hand along the hospital bed.

"Looking my best?" Penney grinned.

"Emotionally vulnerable, is what I was going to say." Colby brushed a damp hair from her cheek. "By the way, you've never looked better to me."

"God, you have low standards." She laughed.

Colby leaned down and kissed her. "They couldn't possibly be higher," he whispered.

"Well, aren't you two a pretty picture," said the nurse, bustling in with the small infant bundle. "She's all yours, if you've got a little of that love to spare."

"No end to it around here," Colby said. The nurse deposited baby Amber in Penney's arms.

Penney looked down at the tiny, pale-faced bundle. The infant had Colby's features, currently melanin-free, but sure to darken up in a matter of days. She'd read about it.

"I think I'm building a whole new batch of love," Penney said. "I can feel it in my heart."

"That'd be your breast milk coming in," the nurse quipped. "Don't get carried away."

Penney stared into Amber's tiny face. "I'm already gone." Her heart trilled with a mix of affection and apprehension. Nothing had ever felt so terrifying. Nothing had ever felt so real.

NOW
April 2024

Cole

Cole regarded his reflection in the hallway mirror. He straightened his bow tie. Not too shabby.

He caught his mom looking at his reflection too.

"Very nice," she said. "Extremely dapper."

"Brewster. Cole Brewster," he said, striking a Bond-like pose.

His mom smiled, her eyes bright with emotion. "That's my boy." She stepped forward and smoothed his lapels. "I can't believe it's your prom night already."

It must have been weird for her, he thought. Seeing him go off to prom. Remembering her own. It must have been super weird.

"Do you wish you'd never had me?" Cole asked her.

"No," Sheryl said. It was as simple as that, and yet it wasn't.

"How can you not regret going to prom with him? Knowing what happened."

Sheryl stood quietly for a moment. "It's not a question of regret, baby. I'm grateful every day that you exist. On some level, sure, I wish there could be a world in which I hadn't been raped but still got to be your mom. But it's an impossible wish, and not something I spend much time thinking about. I believe in looking forward, not back."

Looking forward, Cole thought. *Yes. Let's look forward.*

She smiled sadly. "All the decisions I made felt right at the time. I liked Rob. There was no reason at all to say no when he asked me out. I reported what happened to me. As scary as it was to use my voice in that way, I'm proud that I found the courage to speak up. Keeping you, that was the biggest and hardest choice, but it felt right. It was right. Taking the money instead of taking Rob to court was hard too. It hurt to know I was signing away the truth for a payout, as if I was living up to the accusations of gold-digging. But that money gave us a chance at a decent life. And I doubt if I'd ever have seen Rob behind bars anyway."

Sheryl reached out and grasped Cole's hand. "I'm only sorry that my history means you can't have the relationship with your biological father that you were hoping for."

"Am I like him?" Cole found the courage to ask.

"Only in the best ways. Smart. Charming." She touched his cheek. "Handsome." She turned him back toward the mirror, as if to show him who he was. "But that cold streak, not at all. Not even a little bit."

Cole wasn't so sure. "How can you be sure?"

"Because I know you. I raised you. The way Rob is, was learned, not born."

Perhaps she thought those words would absolve him, but they didn't. They were scary too, after everything Amber had told him about sexism being culturally ingrained.

"You're going to have a wonderful time tonight," Sheryl told him. "I can feel it."

Amber

Amber smoothed the skirt of her Ratliff-approved prom dress and laced her fingers into Carmen's. Her date looked snazzy hot in her tailored tux. Shined shoes, pin-striped pants, matching vest, cut low to accent the generous mounds peeking up between the wings of her unbuttoned dress shirt, and jaunty bow tie resting inside the V of the collar, perfectly tied. She held the jacket by two fingers on her free hand, draping it over her shoulders like a runway model.

"Or," Amber said as they strolled through the parking lot, "we could skip the dance part and go someplace where I can jump your bones."

"Nah." Carmen smiled. "We look way too good to keep it to ourselves."

The dance was being held in the local university ballroom, not exactly the most glamorous setting but still slightly fancier than the homecoming celebration held in the school's own gymnasium.

Entering the building, Amber had flashbacks to being little, following her mom into a job fair. Or racing down to the snack bar in the student union basement, where she'd color at her own table while her mom sat with her study group.

She thought about the night, about eighteen years ago, when her mom must have come in these same doors in a prom dress, hand in hand with her dad, not suspecting it would be their last night of true freedom for a long, long time.

Amber looked over at Carmen. She felt grateful that they could make out and make love—make anything they wanted, really—and not have to worry about making a baby by accident. Someday, it might be nice to be parents, but a long time from now.

Music was already pumping from inside the ballroom. Strains of the eternal classic "I Want You Back" by the Jackson 5 came blasting at them.

"All right," Carmen said. "Starting us out old-school."

"Way old," Amber agreed. She was ready to get her groove on.

The ballroom was decorated in a mix of sickly pink and shocking green. The vowel-challenged cheerleaders greeted them at the door.

"Hiiiii," said Brii.

"Hiiiii," Carmen and Amber responded.

Brii beamed. She had a clipboard. "Names on the ticket?"

"Carmen Vallejo and Amber Harris-Rutledge."

Jyssyca pointed like a flight attendant. "Pictures on the left, snack table on the right."

"Emergency exits?" Amber asked.

Carmen snickered.

Jyssyca tilted her head. "There's this door and then two on either side of the stage."

"Great, thanks," Amber said, holding in her laugh.

"When you leave, don't forget to check out with us and get your prom favors," Abbe said, returning to the apparent script. She waved her hand at the table stacked with neatly packaged plastic bags. Each contained a mug and a piece of cloth that might have been a folded towel or T-shirt or something.

"We won't." Carmen eyed the mountain of prom favor bags, each tied with a curly green and pink ribbon. "It must have been a lot of work to put all this together," she said. "Everything looks great. Thanks."

Abbe's eyes went wide. "SO much work. Thanks." The cheerleaders beamed at them.

Carmen and Amber proceeded toward the dance floor.

Blossom

Blossom straightened Julio's boutonniere as they stood in line at the photo booth. There were two photo stations side by side. The first was a formal spot where each couple could stand, in the frame of the decorative balloon arch amid a veritable garden of white flowers, green vines, and baby's breath. The second was a long ivory backdrop speckled with the school logo, red carpet style. Couples and groups of friends were posing with the large picture frame cutouts, goofy costume accessories, and exclamations on sticks ("Awesome!" "OMG!" "Go, Buford!").

A handful of sophomore A/V club kids were stationed there to help out. They had a pair of real cameras on tripods taking formal pictures, but they were also taking cell photos for people, so it was taking forever to make it to the front of the line.

Julio had his hand on her waist. "I know I've told you this already, but you look exceptionally beautiful tonight."

He had recently discovered that the purple top and the ball gown skirt were two separate items, and his current pastime was to slip his fingers in between to stroke her skin. He leaned his mouth toward hers.

"Don't kiss me now," Blossom said quickly.

"What?" Julio seemed startled.

"Not until after the picture, you doof. I just redid my lipstick and we've been waiting too long to start over."

Julio grinned, clearly relieved. "I'll wait for you as long as it takes, Blossom Morgan."

Cole

"I need to freshen up," Marin said. "Can you handle dancing alone for a minute?"

"Yeah, of course," Cole said. "I'll take a punch and cookie break."

"Ooh, get me one," she said, spinning away.

He headed toward the refreshments table. He smiled at the art teacher who was currently standing guard by the punch bowl. How weird must it be to be at prom as a chaperone, he wondered. The art teacher eyed him suspiciously.

Cole had no plans to spike the punch bowl, but he accepted the fact that he must look the part. Jock-adjacent. Child of a sex offender. Grandchild of two people with drug addictions on one side and on the other side, the sort of people who buy their way out of facing consequences. How many other sketchy boxes did he need to tick to warrant chaperone side-eye?

Tonight, Cole was operating entirely aboveboard and it felt surprisingly good. He'd taken Marin out to dinner, offered her a sip from the flask he'd prepared because he knew she was expecting it and he didn't want to disappoint. But he was going to stay clean tonight.

His mother kept no alcohol in the house. She didn't drink and never had, because she made a choice when she was young to break the cycle of addiction in her family. She probably hoped Cole would follow in her footsteps on that front, and so far he hadn't lived up to that hope. But he could change that. He wasn't sure about forever, but he was sure about tonight.

He could change other cycles, too, he had determined. Amber's little talking-to had helped him see that. If it wasn't cut-and-dried, if it wasn't a foregone conclusion, if being a good guy or a bad guy was entirely a matter of choice, if monsters were made and not born, like Amber and his mother both seemed to think . . . then Cole could be something other than what the man who fathered him had been.

Cole put a scoop of punch into a glass and turned back to face the dance floor. As he did, he happened to spot Emmy bopping at the edge of the crowd. Cole glanced toward the exit. If he knew anything about Marin, she'd be a good long minute in the ladies' room. There was time.

He moved toward the dance floor and tapped Emmy on the shoulder.

"Can I talk to you for a minute?"

Emmy looked hesitant.

"Just here in this room," he said, pointing toward a quiet corner. "It'll only take a minute, I promise."

"Okay," she said, and followed him.

"I wanted to apologize for my behavior the other night. In the car."

"Oh." Emmy nodded. "It's okay."

Cole frowned. "No, I really feel bad about hurting you. And scaring you. I don't want to be like that. Not ever again. I'm really sorry."

"It's okay," she said again.

"I don't think it is, though," Cole said. "I messed up, and I upset you. That's why I wanted you to know that I really do apologize."

"It's okay."

Cole smiled. He couldn't explain to her what he was feeling, or that she didn't have to shrug it off. Not as well as Amber had explained it all to him, anyway. "Well, thanks. It's nice of you to try to make me feel better."

"It's kind of just what guys do, right?" Emmy said. She gazed at him with this bland expression.

That was it. Right then and there. For Cole, that was the lightning bolt. Of how totally messed up the dating culture they'd all internalized could be.

"I want to be better," Cole said. "I'm going to be better. And I wanted you to be the first to know it. Because you deserve better than what happened." No, that was passive. He had to own his actions. "You deserve better than what I did that night, Emmy. And I really do apologize."

"Thanks," she said, smiling. "I feel a little better about it now that you've said that, actually. So, thanks." She offered a small wave and melted away into the dancing crowd.

Amber

Two hours into the dance, the time had come. The band crooned through a slow ballad, bringing the room from a frenzied hopping mob to a calm, swaying forest of sequins and hormones.

"You ready for this?" Carmen asked, her arms looped around Amber's waist.

Amber leaned her head on Carmen's shoulder. "If I get expelled, please remember me fondly."

"She can't expel all of us," Carmen said. "That's the entire point." She leaned down and caught Amber's lips in hers.

As the current song ended, Amber moved toward the stage. She climbed up the stairs to where the lead singer could see her and gave him a little wave.

He nodded. He tore off a quick improv riff on his electric guitar, loud and intense and attention catching enough to settle the room into silence. Then he leaned into the mic.

"And now, it's time for a very special number, going out to a very special administrator, from the entire senior class." The lead singer shaded his eyes and peered into the dark auditorium. "Where's the inimitable Mrs. Ratliff?"

A spotlight clicked on, illuminating a surprised Mrs. Ratliff, standing by the wall near the punch bowl. Everyone cheered.

Perfect. Amber tossed a thumbs-up to the A/V nerds in the rafters. The spotlight was there to highlight the prom king and queen, which had happened a few minutes ago, but Amber had bought an encore with the ease of a cool twenty bucks.

The lead singer pulled a small notecard out of his front pocket. "Mrs. Ratliff, the Buford High seniors would like you to know that they've read and observed the Buford High Prom Dress Code to the absolute letter. And I quote: 'Tuxedos should include: bow tie or necktie, vest or cummerbund, dress shirt, jacket, and optional accessories such as suspenders or cuff links. Shoes and matching socks.'"

He paused, turned the card over, and turned it back. "Uh— that's it, y'all. Did anyone notice one conspicuous item was not mentioned?"

"Why, yes, Chad," said the drummer. "That would be pants."

The entire senior class screamed with delight.

Mrs. Ratliff's jaw dropped.

"So, Mrs. Ratliff, this one's for you!" proclaimed the singer.

The drummer clanged the snare, shouting, "One, two, a-one, two, three, four!" And the band struck into the upbeat rhythm of Hot Chocolate's "You Sexy Thing (I Believe in Miracles)."

As planned, all the seniors began to dance, writhing and gyrating dramatically. Other students scooted out of the way to witness the spectacle. Soon the seniors in dresses were surrounding the seniors in tuxes, forming one large circle. The ring of mostly girls turned to face outward, covering their eyes and gasping as though horrified, in unison.

From inside the ring came the soft sound of fabric shushing. The outer ring continued to gyrate to the "Sexy" lyrics, eyes covered. They did their individual best to channel their inner exotic dancer. Amber pumped her fists alongside her hips, as though thrusting. Beside her Blossom put her hands toward the ground and stuck her shimmying butt in the air, matching Amber's thrusts with tosses of her hair.

Mrs. Ratliff strode forward, approaching the stage. "This is not an approved song!" she shouted to the band. "Stop at once!"

The seniors cheered and howled. The outer ring dispersed, leaving the formerly tux-clad crew exposed. Very exposed— they had all stripped down to their boxers! Each guy still wore a dress shirt, now over nothing but matching black and white tuxedo-styled boxers, complete with a decorative bow tie across the front of the fabric.

"That's right, Mrs. Ratliff," announced the lead singer as the administrator stormed onto the stage. "You forgot to mandate . . . PANTS!"

"Stop at once!" Mrs. Ratliff screeched. "Cease and desist, or I'll see that you won't be paid!"

"Sorry." The lead singer shrugged. "We've already been paid. And our contract allows us to play what we want."

"I submitted the approved list of songs!" Mrs. Ratliff argued.

"And we took it under advisement," the singer responded with a grin. He resumed singing the chorus.

At the side of the stage, Amber crossed her arms smugly.

Mrs. Ratliff stormed over, narrowing her eyes at Amber. "I know this stunt was your doing. This isn't over."

"I quite agree." Amber smiled sweetly. "It's just beginning, Mrs. Ratliff." She waved her hand at the chaos that was the dance floor.

With the lead singer back on the lyrics, the crowd cheered louder. The other students, first transfixed at the fringes, now came forward, joining the fray. Everyone was singing at the top of their lungs. Miracles, indeed.

Mrs. Ratliff growled and charged down the stairs, nearly

bowling over Carmen, who was standing on the floor video-taping the whole thing. Around the room, more of the A/V club had cameras too, taking video clips and snapping stills for the newspaper.

This night had better make the yearbook, Amber thought. It would definitely be next week's front-page headline in the *Buford Bee*, if she had anything to say about it.

When the song ended, Amber bounded down the steps too. The dance floor erupted in cheers.

"Did you get it?" Amber gushed.

Carmen lowered her phone. "Oh yeah. I got it all."

They threw their arms around each other in excitement as the band segued into another upbeat number: WALK THE MOON's "Shut Up and Dance."

Amber and Carmen raced back to the dance floor. The senior guys showed no signs of intent to put their pants back on. In fact, some of the guys who hadn't even known about the protest in advance were stripping down too!

Mrs. Ratliff ran around the room trying to stop the madness, but it was too late. Plus, the boys weren't technically breaking any rules, since the requirement of pants was nowhere in the dress code.

"Amber: one. Patriarchy: zero," Carmen quipped.

"Those are only tonight's stats," Amber lamented.

"You can pick up your sword again on Monday." Carmen dragged her into the midst of the wildly excited dancers.

"It's implied!" Ratliff shrieked, circling back toward them. "'Tuxedo' implies pants!"

"'Tuxedo' implies everything on the list," someone shouted from within the dancing crowd. "Guess your mistake was being too specific."

"And also not specific enough," someone else chimed in.

"Bow ties are still all accounted for!" One guy danced toward Mrs. Ratliff, comically pointing at the design on his boxers.

Mrs. Ratliff screamed in frustration as she stormed off.

Amber threw her hands in the air. Carmen was right. Her work here was done. She could shut up and dance with the best of them, but inside she was glowing, screaming, crowing. This was the best night ever.

The half-naked prom was a go.

Cole

Cole sat at one of the prom tables, scarfing down chips from the mound on his plate. A few feet away, Marin, a little tipsy, was dancing with his friend Alex. They looked like they were on a third date, his hands all up on her.

Cole wanted to leave. There were fifteen minutes left in the dance and he didn't want to experience a one of them. He wanted to put his pants back on and bounce.

Alex wasn't wearing pants either. Marin was not pretending not to notice. She was throwing herself at him. Normally, he would have intervened. She was Cole's date, for crying out loud. But in fairness, normally it wouldn't have gotten to that point because Cole would have been the one on the receiving end.

But an hour ago, Marin had declared him "being weird" and given up. So it was as much his fault as anyone's. Not that there had to be fault, he supposed. Marin could do what she wanted. He didn't own her. And she didn't owe him.

Cole shoveled down more chips.

"Isn't that your girlfriend?" said a girl he didn't recognize.

"Nah, not officially," he said. "But we came together, yeah."

"She's grinding on my prom date."

"Oh, shit." Cole coughed out a laugh. "Sorry. Want me to pull her off him?"

"Nah," the girl said. "We're just friends." She looked toward the door. "Fourteen minutes and counting."

"Tell me about it."

She was pretty. Soft red hair done up in a swirl thing. Pale skin and freckles. He'd hit that.

No. NO. He shook off the thought. She was pretty. He liked the look of her.

"Your hair looks pretty like that," he said.

"Thanks." She touched the loose tendril self-consciously.

"Do we know each other? I'm Cole."

"I don't go here," she said. "I'm Laura. I go to church with Alex."

"Cool."

"Do you have a designated driver?" Laura asked him after they watched Alex and Marin sway for a minute.

"I'm my own designated driver tonight," he said. "I'm so sober it's borderline tragic." He was exaggerating a little. He'd actually had a ton of fun tonight. Seeing Amber's protest come off as a success had been the highlight, surprisingly. He'd danced plenty, too, but in the end it turned out to be less of a giggle to wrangle a drunk girl when you weren't drunk yourself. Things to reflect on.

Laura grinned. "I'm sober too, but we came in a limo. Any chance you'd give me a ride home?" she asked. "I'm pretty sure they're going to be making out in a coat closet before long."

Cole laughed. "Sure," he said. That actually sounded like a huge relief. Laura seemed calm. Confident. She was funny. Not pushy. He waved at Marin.

Marin teetered over, with Alex in tow. "Why aren't you dancing?" she asked.

"My feet got tired," Cole lied. "It looked like you were having fun with Alex, though."

"You're so off tonight," Marin said. "At least Alex is up for some fun."

Alex had his hands on Marin's waist. Cole observed that, then looked at Alex.

"The dance is almost over, and I'm getting ready to leave. And I brought you," Cole said to Marin. "So I should be the one to take you home."

"I wanna stay with Alex," she whined.

Honestly, Cole was fine with that. Alex clearly wanted it too. And he had a limo, so there wasn't an issue with wondering how she'd get home. "Okay, so you stay with Alex and I'll drive Laura home."

Alex leaned in and hugged him, pounding his back. "I owe you a solid, man."

"Sure," Cole said. No reason to admit he was very happy with the deal.

"Where do you live?" he asked Laura as they headed for the coat check. She described the neighborhood. It wasn't exactly on his way. But it *was* on the way to something else.

"I can take you straight there. Unless you want to swing by and check out the cosmic bowling after-party first."

"Really?" she asked. "I actually kinda did want to try that."

Cole grinned. "Okay, then. Could be fun."

"If it's not, we can always bail."

"Just say the word."

"What word? Do we need a code word?" she asked as he helped her into her jacket.

"How about 'get me out of here,'" he suggested. "That way there's no confusion."

"Perfect," Laura said. She cast one last glance at the dance floor as they picked up their party favor bags. "Get me out of here?"

"On it." Cole swept his hand dramatically toward the door and offered a slight bow. They headed out together, laughing.

Maybe the night wasn't a total loss. They'd gotten to stick it to Ratliff and now he was on his way to a kind of date, or something. With someone new. Someone who wouldn't have heard tell of his past doggish tendencies. He was ready to practice turning over his new leaf. And he was excited to practice with Laura.

Amber

"We're viral," Amber said. She lay in Carmen's bed, monitoring the social media feeds and the video views.

"No way," Carmen said, rolling toward her. "Already?"

"Ten thousand views and counting!" Amber exclaimed. "Can you believe it?"

"I can," Carmen said. "It was pretty epic. You actually pulled it off."

"Totally," Amber agreed. "And let's not forget whose brilliant idea it was in the first place. *We* pulled it off."

Carmen smiled. "*We* make a great team." She winked. "Me, the brains. You, the brawn . . ."

Amber frowned. "Hey. Who you callin' brawny?"

"You do pick things up quick . . ." Carmen laughed.

Amber joined her. "I suggest you quit while you're ahead," she said, leaning her cheek on Carmen's shoulder. "If you don't start kissing me soon, I might hatch a plot to take over the world."

"Please," Carmen said, wrapping her arms around Amber. "That sounds like a Monday problem."

"Agreed," Amber said, as their mouths met.

Blossom

Julio cracked open the bottle of sparkling cider and poured it into two plastic champagne flutes. He pulled the plate of chocolate-covered strawberries from the mini fridge. He'd planned his heart out to make the evening romantic, including checking into the hotel room in the late afternoon to deliver the snacks and a nice bouquet of flowers.

"Some champagne for the lady?" he offered now.

"That sounds lovely." Blossom accepted the flute of cider with a smile.

Julio knelt beside her on the bed and set the plate of strawberries between them. "Happy prom night, Blossom."

They clinked glasses to toast, then sipped. She tipped her chin up and he kissed her. For a moment, their locked lips took precedence over the strawberries and cider.

"Will they or won't they?" Blossom joked as they pulled apart, affecting the tone of a TV announcer. "Fans near and far are at the edge of their seats, wondering."

Julio grinned. "I better not see any of this on pay-per-view later."

"Why? You don't think we'd be porno-worthy on our first time? That's not what a girl wants to hear."

"You're . . . not normal," he said, raising an eyebrow at her.

Blossom laughed. "That's not what a girl wants to hear, either."

Julio looked at the ceiling. "See, I feel like I'd get in equally as much trouble for trying to tell you what you want to hear. Like I'm manipulating you or being disingenuous, or something."

"Ooh, 'disingenuous,'" Blossom cooed. "That *is* what I want to hear. Deploy that big vocabulary, baby. Makes me hot for you."

"Improbable," Julio said. "Surely it's my pectoralis major and my latissimus dorsi that have you going, not to mention my biceps brachii." He raised his fist to make a muscle, showing off his arm, chest, and shoulder.

"Brains and brawn. How yummy."

"Ever redoubtable, Blossom."

"LOL. 'Redoubtable.' That sounds sketch."

"It means—"

"I know what it means. It means you were the spelling bee champion four years in a row in elementary school."

"And I have the blue-ribbon trophies to prove it. So what are we going to do?"

Blossom spread her arms against the headboard. "I don't know."

"Do you want me to take you home?" Julio asked.

"No, I want to stay with you. I want us to do . . . something."

"How far do you want to take it?"

"I don't know yet. All I know is that you're cute, and you're standing too far away from me."

Julio shifted his weight. "I'm nervous."

"Me too."

"Okay. So should we wait?"

Waves of disappointment washed over her. "If you want. Is that what you want?"

"No, I want us to do . . . something." Julio knelt on the end of the bed.

"So, come over here." Blossom smiled, fanning the ends of her long hair with her fingers. "And let's see what happens."

THEN
February 2006

Mina/Penney/Sheryl

Sunday brunch. The first of many, though it wasn't yet a formalized tradition. That day, it was the three tired moms of three snoozing infants, spooning Chinese delivery into their faces and talking quietly, hoping not to wake the babies.

"I just want to say," Sheryl started. "I really appreciate this space that we're making together."

Penney raised her mug of tea. "Here's to our new home," she said.

Sheryl nodded. "It hasn't felt like home to me anywhere in a long time."

"We're going to change that," Mina promised, raising her glass, too. "The babies are already changing it."

"The home is where the poop pail is," Penney joked.

They laughed together.

"I've been trying for a long time to make peace with the family I was born into," Sheryl said. "But now I see, there's a different way. Here's to the family we choose."

NOW

April 2024

Amber/Blossom/Cole

Sunday brunch. Nowhere near the first and certainly not the last, but simply one unique moment in time. The celebrations of one unique family.

"We pulled it off!" Amber declared. "And we're up to a hundred thousand views online."

"How many of those viewers were *you?*" Cole quipped.

Amber grabbed a slice of baguette out of the bread basket and tossed it at him. He caught it with one hand, winked at her, and took a bite.

"That's amazing," Blossom exclaimed. "That'll show Ratliff who's boss."

"Pretty sure Amber is staring down a lifetime in detention come Monday," Cole said. "It was nice knowing ya, sis."

"Why should Amber get in trouble?" piped up little Diamond. "She didn't even take off her pants."

Amber ruffled her baby sister's curly hair. "That's exactly right, D."

"You were, ahem, the ringleader," Cole reminded her. "And it's not as if Ratliff can put the whole senior class in detention."

"We'll be sure to slip you some paper and a pencil during visitation hours," Blossom joked. "Your next article can be about your wrongful imprisonment."

"It could," Amber mused. "Who knew you could be a political prisoner in your own high school?"

"The headline writes itself," Cole declared.

Everybody laughed.

"In all seriousness," Mina said. "You all do know we're proud of you?"

Penney nodded. "It takes guts to stand up for what you believe in."

"Definitely. It takes balls," Colby said. "And I'm gathering that there were plenty on display last night."

They all laughed again. "Oh, my god, Dad," Amber groaned. "Stahp."

"He's right," Penney chimed. "Someone had to air that dirty laundry."

"Y'all are disgusting," Amber howled.

Sheryl pretended to consult her cell phone. "As of this morning, the Wikipedia entry for 'the boxer rebellion' has disambiguation notes at the top."

"Bwa-ha-ha, Mama," Cole said, offering a slow clap.

"Sheryl wins nerdiest reference," Mina declared. "Which I find personally offensive."

"You know what I find personally offensive?" Colby started.

"Nope, eww, nope." Amber leaped up from the table. "I don't wanna hear it, Dad. Time for dessert. Anyone?" She started picking up people's empty plates.

Still laughing, Blossom and Penney got up along with her to help with the clearing.

"So?" Penney whispered.

"Surely you're not going to ask me to spill details in front of him," Blossom whispered back. Julio was seated at the table, laughing and joking along with the rest of the crowd. Blossom knew Penney had been furtively glancing at the pair all through the meal, trying to gauge if anything had changed between them.

Amber went back to clear more. They were alone in the kitchen. Penney corralled Blossom near the sink. With the water running, no one could hear. "Thumbs up, thumbs down, at least? Throw a mom a bone."

"Nah, you're gonna have to live in suspense on this one." Blossom smiled sweetly. "Since I'm your favorite and all."

"Your stock is dropping rapidly." Penney smirked. "Anyway, I have my suspicions."

"Suspish all you want," Blossom said airily. "My lips are sealed."

"Or are they?" Penney muttered, smiling to herself.

Blossom grinned innocently and fled to the safety of the crowded table.

"A series of bad dad jokes," Amber informed her. "Be glad you were spared."

"Hey," Colby said. "I like to think I'm a great dad."

"It's not a binary," Cole and Amber said in unison. Surprised, she glanced at him. They shared a quiet smile.

"Pie is served," Penney announced, waltzing in with a pecan pie in one hand and chocolate chess pie in the other. "Get it while it's gelatinous!"

Blossom glanced around the table at the faces of all her loved ones. They were lucky, she knew. She and Cole and Amber, especially. The fact that all three of them existed and were still all here together—it was a lightning strike. One incredibly rare possibility out of the millions of possible universes they could occupy. The confluence of uncountable moment-by-moment decisions. Three in particular.

Blossom raised her glass. "Hey, we never did toast," she said. "To surviving prom night in style?"

"Heck, yeah," Amber said. "In STYLE."

Cole raised his glass alongside theirs. He looked around the table at all the smiling faces. He looked at his mom, repeating something he'd heard her say more than once. "Here's to making the best of the family we're born with," he said. "And to cherishing the family we choose."

Reflections and Resources

The first spark of the idea for this book hit me almost ten years ago. Then I began to actually sit down and write it about five years ago, which means that in the time I spent researching and writing the novel, the landscape of reproductive freedom in the United States changed significantly.

Back in 2015, abortion was legal throughout the country. The 1973 U.S. Supreme Court ruling in *Roe v. Wade* declared that a pregnant person's right to privacy in making medical decisions outweighed the state's right to control individual behavior. But in 2022 a new Supreme Court ruling in *Dobbs v. Jackson* overturned *Roe v. Wade*, ending fifty years of protection for reproductive freedom.

Exploring teen pregnancy through the lens of fiction felt one way when abortion was legal for all. Now, it feels slightly different. The very idea of choosing to follow through with an unplanned pregnancy takes on new meaning when the aspect of choice has been removed for many people.

I believe in each pregnant person's right to choose what is right for them, their body, and their own life, as well as the potential life they are carrying. Some people choose abortion, some choose adoption, and some choose parenthood. The three pregnant characters in this book, Mina, Penney, and Sheryl, each chose to carry their pregnancy to term and keep their baby. This is only one of several valid choices they could have made.

If you or someone you know is struggling with decisions related to sex, relationships, pregnancy, or parenthood, there are many resources available to support you. The list of organizations below offers a place to begin:

PLANNED PARENTHOOD: plannedparenthood.org

REPRODUCTIVE FREEDOM FOR ALL: reproductivefreedomforall.org

CENTER FOR REPRODUCTIVE RIGHTS: reproductiverights.org

This book also features a character who experiences sexual assault. For resources and support related to rape or sexual assault, check out these organizations:

NATIONAL SEXUAL ASSAULT HOTLINE: 1-800-656-HOPE (1-800-656-4673)

RAINN: rainn.org is the nation's largest anti-sexual violence organization. RAINN created and operates the National Sexual Assault Hotline in partnership with more than one thousand local sexual assault service providers across the country.

When our individual freedoms are limited by law, it puts us all at risk. To find out how to use your voice to advocate for reproductive freedom for all, First Amendment rights to freedom of speech and expression, and other individual freedoms, check out these organizations:

ADVOCATES FOR YOUTH: advocatesforyouth.org works alongside thousands of young people in the U.S. and around the globe as they fight for sexual health, rights, and justice. Their reproductive freedom project is known as **ABORTION OUT LOUD** (advocatesforyouth.org/abortion-out-loud/).

AMERICAN CIVIL LIBERTIES UNION (ACLU): aclu.org works in courts, legislatures, and communities to defend and preserve our constitutional rights and liberties. They advocate for reproductive rights and freedom of expression (e.g., confronting school dress codes), among other important issues.

ACKNOWLEDGMENTS

Thanks to the young activists around the country and around the world who speak up and fight for reproductive rights, social justice, and freedom of expression for all. Keep up the good work!

Thanks to my family and friends for supporting my work and providing counsel and encouragement as I considered the myriad complex issues that came up in the writing process. I'm especially grateful to Cynthia Smith, Emily Kokie, Nicole Valentine and Lexie R., Karen Meisner, and Alice Dodge for sharing their thoughts on this project.

Thanks to my editor, Kate Farrell, as well as Valery Badio, Nicole Banholzer, Julia Bianchi, Molly Ellis, Chantal Gersch, Sarah Gompper, Samira Iravani, Linda Minton, Alexandra Quill, Mary Van Akin, Ann Marie Wong, and the entire publishing team at Macmillan, for their work to turn the manuscript into a book and send it out into the world.

Thanks to my agent, Ginger Knowlton—she's the best!

Thanks to the many teachers, librarians, administrators, legislators, school boards, and community members who are fighting to keep books with diverse characters and books about challenging and controversial subject matter available in their local schools and libraries. Their work is vital because the conversations sparked by these texts can change lives, and even sometimes save them.

Finally, thanks to all the wonderful readers out there. Go forth and raise your voice!